Dedicated to the memory of Captain Ryan Anderson,
who gave his life for this country.

IT'S OVER KILL

IT'S OVER KILL

M. Alex Harris

Spotted Ranch Books LLC
Chino Valley, Arizona

ISBN 978-1-7327816-0-3

First Edition
Printed in the United States of America

Contents

Chapter 1	1
Chapter 2	10
Chapter 3	26
Chapter 4	29
Chapter 5	33
Chapter 6	36
Chapter 7	42
Chapter 8	49
Chapter 9	53
Chapter 10	58
Chapter 11	61
Chapter 12	65
Chapter 13	72
Chapter 14	78
Chapter 15	81
Chapter 16	90
Chapter 17	94
Chapter 18	97
Chapter 19	101
Chapter 20	107

1

THE DUST SETTLED as Chalcey dismounted Red, the Pony Of America (POA). Red stood 12 hands; his markings matched an Appaloosa's and he was the prettiest shade of rust. Chalcey had found him at a horse rescue a few months earlier and the horse and girl had immediately bonded. Red was truly the reason she was getting over the untimely death of her father.

"I swear, Chalcey," Summer laughed, "soon we'll have to put you on a real horse."

"Summer, don't you talk bad about Red. And I'll never outgrow him, even when I am as old as you, I won't caste him aside. He'll always have a place with me." Anders Chalcedony Wolfe put her hands on her hips and responded to her great grandmother Summer Bear and then put her arms around Red's neck. Tall like her mother, grandmother and great grandmother, Chalcey thrust her chin out in defiance and in jest. Chalcey's red hair was almost a perfect match for Red's mane and tail. People who saw them together sometimes said she must color her hair to match her horse. But those people didn't know Chalcey or Summer or they would have known better.

"Come on Chalcey, brush him down, hang up your tack and let's go get supper." Chalcey's great grandmother instructed her, knowing occasionally Chalcey forgot to hang up the tack.

"What about feeding everybody else?" Chalcey was concerned

about the other three horses, the pig, goat, chickens, raccoon, not to mention the dogs and cats. Chalcey had brought one cat, rescued another, found a mistreated dog at the pound, and on a ride found a baby raccoon whose mama had been run over.

"It can wait til after supper honey. Shake a leg." Summer prodded Chalcey and walked off to the ranch house.

Summer had lived on the ranch long before it became known as Bear Ranch. Back in 1954, Summer took over when both of her parents were killed in a car accident and she changed her name to Summer Bear. Bear Ranch wasn't the largest ranch, but Summer had taken great pains to make it successful and self-sustaining over the years. She built the barn, and tack shed with help from her first husband, who died at the wheel of their combine. Then Summer married again and husband number two helped fence and cross fence the 15 acres, put in two wells, brought in solar power and put in stock tanks. Since Bear Ranch backed up to the national forest, it was like owning half of Yavapai County. Nearly everyone in Prescott knew of Summer and those who knew her personally always called her Summer, even her daughter, granddaughter, and great granddaughter.

Chalcey clomped into the recently remodeled kitchen that has served thousands of meals and people, the look on her face could only be described as petulant, "Summer why do we always do all the work? Why doesn't Oriole or Marlowe have to help?"

"Honey, what brought that up?" Summer stopped stirring the homemade stew and laid down the spoon while turning to her only great granddaughter.

"Well, you cook and clean, I muck the stalls and feed all the critters twice a day and go to school and do 4-H and you teach classes. Marlowe just goes to the office and Oriole just goes to work. Why can't they help us more?"

Summer sat at the huge oak dining table with a glass of ice tea for herself and Chalcey. "Your mama works hard and many long hours and she does more than her fair share—on her days off she feeds and mucks too, and every other weekend she takes rotation to cook dinner. Now, Marlowe does the same, but hers is a little different. Both your mama and grandma keep this place going by paying the mortgage and upkeep. Why I'd have lost the place if not for the two of them. And you'd be living in the city without old Red. Darling, are you feeling kinda overwhelmed with all the chores and schoolwork? Is that what's going on?" Summer watched her great granddaughter's face as the inquiry soaked in. She could see Chalcey processing the question.

Tears welled up in Chalcey's eyes. "I don't want to sound ungrateful. Summer, you and Marlowe have been great to Mama and me. I've never lived in such a great place and being able to have Red & Buttercup & Popeye & Puddles. Maybe I'm feeling lonely maybe I miss my Dad and want Mama around like other kids have their mama's and dad's."

"Chalcey, those are words well beyond your years", Summer's analysis into Chalcey's pain and heartache brought her up short.

"Come on, let's set the table and you go change for supper."

The emotional overflow forgotten momentarily, Chalcey asked to use the good crystal, silver and china. "But, Chalcey, it's just homemade stew and biscuits and cucumber salad."

"I know, but the good stuff always makes me feel special." Chalcey gave her great grandmother that tilt of her head and the smile that has tugged at Summer's heart since Chalcey was born. "OK. Let's get out the good stuff and the nice Irish linen too."

Marlowe and Oriole drove in the yard almost simultaneously just as the sun was setting. The Mercedes contrasted with Oriole's Jeep 4 wheel drive, in color and style. Marlowe's success as an attorney was evident in the cream colored Mercedes she drove for work. Oriole drove a four year old bright red 4 wheel drive Jeep for comfort and practicality.

"Hey, Marlowe, spring any of my cases?" Oriole asked her attractive mother.

"Oriole, don't you start on me today. I've asked them not to give me any cases you've worked on and it seems to be pretty consistent. Since they've assigned you to the Verde and me to Prescott. I don't see your name in any of my files." Marlowe swatted her tall skinny daughter with her briefcase as they walked up the steps arm in arm.

"Summer, Chalcey, we're home. Hey, where is everybody?"

"In the kitchen. Supper in 10 minutes. Hot biscuits in the oven. Wash up. Chalcey is serving." Marlowe and Oriole looked at each other quizzically as Summer finished her rendition.

Whispering to her mom, Oriole said, "What's that all about. Chalcey would rather eat than serve."

Oriole and Marlowe joined Summer and Chalcey in the huge

county kitchen. Marlowe poured a glass of Gewurztraminer and nodded to Oriole to see if Oriole wanted one. Oriole shook her head "no thanks, on call tonight."

"Chalcey, how was your day," Oriole put her arms around her gangly red haired daughter.

Chalcey hugged her mom. "I miss Dad." Oriole looked at Summer over Chalcey's head.

"I know, I miss him too. Come on while I change my clothes and lock up my gun. Let's talk about it." Oriole and Chalcey went up to Oriole's bedroom on the second floor.

"Summer, what happened to make Chalcey bring up Jim. She seemed to have adjusted so well. I haven't heard word one from her for over six months." Marlowe leaned against the refrigerator and sipped her wine.

"She came in from feeding Red and started in. We talked some, but I think this is something her mom needs to help her through. Maybe we all need to be more sensitive to Chalcey's need for a dad. It just seems so strange since my dad was gone, your's gone, Oriole's and now Chalcey's. Are the women in this family cursed or blessed?"

"Summer, I'm too tired to try to analyze all the emotional woes of this family right now. Maybe tomorrow Chalcey and I can go fishing out at Watson Lake."

Summer, Oriole and Marlowe were seated around the oak dining table as Chalcey served the stew and biscuits. Everyone complimented her steady hand and proper etiquette. Just as they finished the main course, Oriole's cell phone rang. She got up from the table to take the call.

"Oriole is on call. That means she'll be gone all night again." Chalcey almost teared up again.

"Chalcey if Mama has to leave maybe we can all play poker until she gets back, since there is no school tomorrow. Let's make a big bowl of popcorn and lemonade and break out the rolls of pennies. OK?" Marlowe reached out to Chalcey and pulled her into a gentle hug.

"Ok. Marlowe, let's feed the critters and then we can come back and help Summer with dishes and then I'll whup you at poker." Chalcey's mood changed rapidly with the promise of a game of penny poker with two of the most cut-throat poker players she knew.

Chapter 1

Oriole came back to the kitchen, "Chalcey, I gotta go. I'm detective on call and they found a body. You mind Summer and Marlowe and don't stay up too late and no cheating you two. Don't be teaching Chalcey bad habits."

Summer and Marlowe looked at each other with mock innocence, "who us?"

Oriole got her emergency bag from the hall closet which contained Vicks, energy bars, water, rain coat, rubber boots, extra clothes and batteries. "See you when I see you. Don't wait up. It might be an all nighter." Oriole had written down directions to Clark Spring Trail, one of the more beautiful little known sights off Iron Springs. It would take about 20 minutes from the ranch. Oriole processed what she knew from dispatch–partially decomposed male body off the trail, one mile from the parking lot.

When she arrived, she saw the patrol deputy, the Medical Examiner's wagon, forensic techs, fire and ambulance, plus some looky-loos.

"Evening Oriole, sorry you got the call." Richard Yellowhorse greeted her as she stepped out of the Jeep. "Fire stepped in and out to announce. Perimeter set up. It's hard to determine what could be the crime scene and its getting on toward dark so I shut down the lot and trail. ME's waiting for you. You're lead on this, so what do you want me to do next?"

"Good job, Yellowhorse. Did you leave anything for me to do?" Oriole smiled with affection at the deputy who had started out as a tribal police officer and recently moved over to the Sheriff's Patrol. Yellowhorse tipped his head in obvious embarrassment. Yellowhorse was a full blood Yavapai Apache living off the reservation in Prescott Valley with his wife and two teen age boys. Yellowhorse practiced Native American traditions and attended St. Anne's Catholic Church every chance he had with his crazy work schedule. A handsome man at 45, with coal black hair turning gray in the temples and not an ounce of fat anywhere on his lean 6'2" frame.

"Just doing my job, detective."

"Who found the body?"

"That kid and his girlfriend over there. They're both pretty shook up. I took the initial statement and called fire. The paramedic walked in, announced, then walked out to wait for the rest. I got all the pertinent info from the kids. Do you want to interview them now or later?"

"Let's get it over with now and see if we can release them, then go on up. Give me the details."

"John Smith, right off his driver's license, swear to God, and Melanie Gruber. They arrived at 5:30, ate their picnic dinner at the benches over there. That SUV is registered to him. No other cars were in the lot. Then they took off for a late afternoon hike. After about a mile, he had to take a leak, oops sorry, answer call of nature. He walked off the trail about 20 feet. He smelled decomp and thought it was an animal. He went to investigate and found the body. They ran back to the car and grabbed his cell phone and called dispatch. They both live in Prescott. Students at Prescott College. No wants or warrants. Got phone numbers and addresses."

Oriole walked over to where the kids were waiting. "Mr. Smith, my name is Oriole Wolfe. I'm a detective with the Sheriff's Office. Could you tell me what happened?"

John Smith's story replicated what Yellowhorse had already told her and Melanie didn't have anything else to add, so Oriole released them to go home and provide a written statement the next day.

"Detective Wolfe, good to see you again." Dr. Rodney Culpepper greeted Oriole. Culpepper appeared to be a hundred years old, but was more like 60, white Einstein hair, full beard, stooped shoulders, and crackling blue eyes. His hobby of raising orchids had made him world famous. His passion for the delicate blooms took him through the inhumanity to man he witnessed daily and it served to provide him with lots of female companionship from fellow garden club members.

"Doc. How's the prize winning orchids?"

"You always remember, don't you? Entered them at the garden show and got first."

"Shall we hike up the hill and see what we can before dark settles in. Hey, Yellowhorse, will you please request some spots. It's going to get dark real fast."

It made a peculiar sight, the ME, the paramedics, the officers trooping up the trail loaded down with bags for the investigation. By the time they arrived at the crime scene tape, there was some heavy breathing going on. Oriole pulled out the Vicks and passed it around to quell the smell of the decomposing flesh.

"Doc, I'm starting the tape recorder. John, go ahead and start with the digital camera. Yellowhorse, you run the camcorder."

"Approximately twenty feet off the trail in a NE direction I see what appears to be a male, on his left side. Unknown age. However, it appears there has been some animal activity. We'll need to cordon this off and do a step search in daylight. Sufficient debris, cigarette butts, cans—soda and beer, wrappers. All that needs to be collected, probably tomorrow. Need to post a deputy overnight right here on the trail. Walking in, in paramedic's footsteps. Smell is moderate, but certainly decomp. Attired in blue jeans, work boots with distinctive tread, snap front shirt looks pretty torn up. Facial hair, looks like a full beard. From what I can see looks like gray hair. That's about it, pause tape and cameras."

The ME knelt on a plastic tarp to get a better look at the body, opened up his bag and began the examination. "Decomp fairly significant, I'd say he's been dead at least four days. No way to tell if this is the primary crime scene until daylight. Looks like scavengers have been at his hands and face. Get pictures from every angle. We won't know more until we roll him over. Bob, give me a hand here, let's roll him over."

Doc Culpepper and Bob rolled the body onto its back. "Uh, oh. Missing left hand too. That's odd. Record. Body's missing left and right hand. Definite signs of animal activity, but how did they get the left hand the way the body was laying on its side. Bob, bag the arms. Let's get him onto the tarp and into the bag. Tomorrow, Oriole, you need to get a search going for the hands. We got pack rats, coyote, bobcats, and no telling what else to contend with." The ME stood up, took off his gloves, deposited them into the evidence bag and turned to leave. "Oriole, I'll probably post him tomorrow at 1:30. You'll be there?"

"I'll be there. Yellowhorse, would you call dispatch for a night watch on the site. Maybe a couple of the volunteers. Be sure they know what to do and what not to do. I'm going back to the office and start a search of missing persons state wide. Doc, how old do you guess?"

"Hard to say, at least 40 based on the hair and body shape. I'd say you are safe doing a 35 to 60 search. White male. Some kind of laborer, well maybe delete that since we can't see his hands. I'd guess 6', 190-200 lbs. Gray, blond hair, full facial beard. That's about all I can give you right now."

Oriole, the ME, tech, and paramedics left. Yellowhorse stayed behind to wait for the volunteers to arrive and keep watch. Yellowhorse wasn't too keen on hanging out where the spirit of the man might be. As he waited he called for his spirit animal to join him. He turned to the East, and called for Mother Earth and Father Sun to protect him. Having enlisted his spirit guides, he sat down in the middle of the trail and waited for the volunteers to arrive.

Oriole arrived back at the office at 11:20. Knowing how long the poker games at Bear Ranch could run, she put in a call. "Summer, whose winning?"

"Have you been coaching Chalcey? She's up $3.57. Marlowe is yawning and fading fast. But that kid is still going strong." Turning away from the game, Summer asked, "What can you tell me?"

"Not too much yet. I'll be home in a couple of hours. Maybe you should just lose, so Chalcey will go to bed. I thought Marlowe was taking her fishing tomorrow."

"Lose! I never throw a game. If she wins, it's because she can. We'll probably be up when you get here."

"I shoulda known. OK, Summer see you a few. Bye."

"Bye, honey, drive safely. Love you."

"Summer why do you always say that to Oriole, Marlowe and me?"

"Oh, Chalcey, it just comes naturally. When your great, great grandma and grandpa left and didn't return, I realized how tenuous life was and I didn't ever want to miss an opportunity to tell those I love that I loved them. Oriole and Marlowe and you are important to me. I love all of you and never want you to forget it. And I never want to wake up to losing someone without having expressed what they meant to me. Now, let's play or go to bed. Which?"

"So what you're saying is I shouldn't let my anger get in the way of telling Oriole I love her when she leaves for work. Gotcha. Think I could call Oriole back and tell her I love her too?"

"Sure."

Chalcey dialed the sheriff's office for her mother. "Hi, Oriole."

"Chalcey, what's going on?"

"Oriole I just wanted you to know I love you. Drive safely, ok. And come kiss me goodnight when you get in. I know I was mad that you had to leave and I apologize."

"Oh, Chalcey, I love you too. I'll come say goodnight when I get there." Oriole's eyes overflowed and she hung up. Thinking out loud Oriole said, "How does that girl do it. One minute you could throttle her and the next she melts your heart. OK, let's get this done and get home." Oriole's search turned up 7 possibles across the state, but none that looked promising. She turned off the computer, turned out the lights and checked out.

Oriole drove home to the ranch pondering the identity of the man found. When she arrived at home, she put her bag back in the hall closet, checked the kitchen to see if the poker game was still going (which it wasn't), locked up and went to Chalcey's room to kiss her goodnight.

"I heard you come in. How was it tonight?" Chalcey asked her mom.

"Chalcey, I think living here has been good for both of us. Summer's compassion is rubbing off on you and me. Thanks for asking about tonight. It's sad. So what are you and Marlowe doing tomorrow?" Oriole changed the direction of the conversation as rapidly as she could without discounting Chalcey's concerns.

"I think we're going fishing. Marlowe and I haven't been fishing for a long time. It'll be fun even if we don't catch anything. Summer said she'd make us a lunch. I think you need to get to bed and get some sleep."

"Who's the mom here?"

"Well, I have lots of examples to learn from, you, Marlowe and Summer. So maybe I'll take my turn." Chalcey smiled at her mother mischievously.

"OK, little mother go to sleep. I won't be getting up too early, so if you take off with Marlowe, remember she's the adult, listen to what she has to say."

2

AT 1:30, Oriole joined Culpepper at the Morgue. She got out her camera, recorder and notepad. She said a short prayer for the soul of the man lying on the stainless steel table.

"Ready, nose plugged with Vicks, Oriole?" Culpepper smiled knowing her seven years as a detective had taught her well.

"Even Vicks won't cover the smell." Oriole steeled herself to continue.

"OK. Let's do it. Preliminary visual—white male, 6'1", 195 pounds. Shirt torn in chest area and sleeves, snaps not buttons, top two snaps undone, shirt untucked in front, but tucked in back. Pants zipped, no wallet or ID in pockets. Steel toed work boots, size 13, covered with some kind of fine gravel or dirt. We'll need samples. No t shirt. Underwear blue boxers, socks heavy white cotton. Scar on abdomen—possible appendectomy. Both hands missing at the wrist. Need microscopic examination. Initial assessment animal activity. Tattoo on left forearm, anchor. Missing big toe on left foot. Decomp set in. Two holes in chest, one through and through. Almost a straight on. Looks like a 9 mm. We'll see if we can retrieve the one inside. No bullet loose in his clothing. So we're missing the 2nd one. Pause recording. Oriole, you've got what looks like a homicide. I'll get you the bullet as soon as I can and diagram the path of the bullets. But it looks like the shots were straight on to the heart and 5 cm to the left center. I'll forward the rest of the findings as soon as I'm done. I'll see if we have any stomach contents and any trace evidence other than the boots. We'll do a lab analysis of the blood. Why don't you go on back to the office with that much. I'll call you as soon as I'm done here."

Oriole left the ME and drove back to the office in Prescott even though she was officially assigned to the Verde office. She briefed her lieutenant with what she had found at the autopsy and the crime scene. "I'm getting ready to go back out there to see if we can locate the hands and any other evidence. There was a lot of garbage strewn along the trail. I suggest we bag it all and determine later what is and isn't evidence." Oriole had been well trained on homicide investigation by the sheriff's office and long discussions with Marlowe on her defense cases.

Oriole left the office and returned to the crime scene. Volunteers had been recruited to grid walk the area looking for animal sign and the missing hands. The volunteers had bagged all the cans and bottles, wrappers, cigarette butts and made castes of any tracks found. Oriole looked at the evidence list, but couldn't find any reference to hand bones. The forensic techs had collected, tagged, and logged every piece of anything they could find. Oriole spoke to Yellowhorse who had been relieved shortly after 2:00 a.m. and gone home to get a couple hours sleep. "Yellowhorse, we need to spread out to see if we can find any pack rat nests or any other critter activity. Will you coordinate that please?"

"Oriole, we have searched about 200 yards in a circle grid. We didn't find pack rats or anything else. Those hands aren't here anywhere. I'm not one to give up, but I think we have to."

"Before we do, let's see if Culpepper has anything more for us." Oriole took out her cell phone and called the ME.

"Any updates, Rod?"

"Do you have a camera in here watching me? I was just getting ready to call you. It looks like the hands were hacked off, no animal bite marks on the bones. Looks more like something with jagged teeth. There is some activity on the flesh but that could be ants, bugs, or rats. I'll know more later. I don't think you're going to find the hands out there. Looks like the hands were removed post mortem and looks to me like the body was placed out there after death. That would take something to move a 200 lb man dead weight. So look for wheel marks like an ATV or wheelbarrow. Are there any tracks recorded?"

Oriole looked at the evidence log and noted the footprints and wheel tracks the volunteers had cast in plaster. "Plenty of footprints and wheel tracks."

"I don't think you'll find his footprints. Have them make photos of everything they found and send over so I can for sure eliminate his boots. Talk to you later." Culpepper signed off in his curt efficient manner.

Oriole confirmed that all footprints were cast as well as all tire prints. It would be a monumental task given the number of mountain bikes and hikers who used the path. She called her partner, Fred O'Neill, to check on progress with the missing persons she had found the night before.

"Wolfe, get your ass back here, we think we have a match given the scars, tats, and missing toe. Marvin Stutz—that's S T U T Z. His daughter reported him missing day before yesterday. He was supposed to meet her for dinner on Tuesday at the Hassayampa Inn. He never showed. She went out to his house. No one there. His truck was gone. Place was locked up tight. She went home. Tried to call him repeatedly. Then she started getting worried. He was in charge of the Chino Pipeline. So she went back out there to see if he was at work. No one there had seen him since Tuesday about 5:30 p.m. At first, she thought maybe he was spending the night with a new friend or something. Then she started getting worried cause he didn't answer his cell. That's when she turned in the missing person. We can go interview her as soon as you get back here." Fred O'Neill hung up leaving Oriole to stare at the phone in her hand.

Arriving back at the office in Prescott, Oriole checked in with Fred. "Are you ready? What's the address for the daughter? You driving or me?"

"I'm driving. I want to get there in one piece. You always drive hell bent for leather." Fred responded. He was the best partner she could have asked for, nearly 20 years her senior, a few inches shorter than her, barrel chested, stocky, precise in his attire; he always wore a Resistol, he hand shaped to his satisfaction and a bolo, the Arizona tie. Fred O'Neill was a died in the wool cowboy cop. He believed in God, Country, and Justice. He'd been a detective for more than 12 years, before that he patrolled the country side putting the bad guys in jail.

Oriole and Fred arrived at Marlene Stutz's condo at 2:30. It was one of the upscale places constructed to look like a Southwestern home all by itself, but in actuality it was connected to other condos. The going price for a condo in that area was a quarter of a million. Oriole took in the sculpted landscaping, the similarity between each residence, the peaceful neighborhood and the fact that no one seemed at home anywhere.

"How do you want to do this?" Fred asked.

"You take the lead. I'll follow." Oriole suggested.

Fred rang the door bell and waited as the door opened. "Ms Stutz, my name is Fred O'Neill, I'm a detective with the Sheriff's Office. This is Detective Wolfe. May we come in?"

Marlene Stutz stood in the doorway. To the detectives, it appeared as if she was trying to process information that could only break her heart. She was short, a little on the fluffy side, dark brown hair to her shoulders. Her appearance was enhanced by the obviously expensive pant suit of teal blue matching her eyes that were too blue made that way by color contacts. She wore 4" heels seemingly to compensate for lack of height. Her eyes were red and bloodshot. In her left hand, she carried wadded up tissue and in her right hand was a glass of white wine. Finally, she snapped out of her stupor and invited the detectives in to a living room that had to be created by one of the hotshot "designers". The carpet was off white, the couch and love seat were a shade up from off white. The walls were Navajo White, with nearly every spare inch covered with a painting done by local artists, some of which Oriole recognized as Neilsen, Coe and Johnston. On the floor in front of the 6' couch was Navajo rug that had to worth $5,000. The coffee table was of hand carved mesquite that Oriole recognized by an artist from Tucson. On the window high bookcase was a Remington Bronze of a cowboy, that had to be worth another $3000. The house had an unlived in feeling. More like a showcase than a home. The woman standing before the detectives looked more like a realtor showing the place than the lady of the house.

"I'm sorry detectives, can I get you something to drink, coffee, tea, or wine?"

"No thanks, ma'am, we're fine." Fred looked at Marlene thinking this woman is already mourning and we haven't even determined it's her father. "Perhaps we could all sit down. We're here to talk about the missing person report."

"Thank God, someone is going to do something. Daddy has been missing for days. I called the Sheriff's Office, the Prescott

Police Department and DPS. No one wants to do anything. They keep saying I'm overwrought. Well, I want you to know I'm not overwrought. I know something has happened. Daddy would never miss dinner with me. We had a standing dinner engagement every week. We used it as a business meeting and family update. I just know something has happened. Daddy would never not call me if he couldn't make it. Not that he never didn't make it. He always made it. He would never stand me up. He was always on time or early. Something dreadful has happened. I just know it." Marlene stopped long enough to drain her glass of white wine. Fred and Oriole looked at each other, Fred did that thing of raising his right eyebrow to say 'hey there's something going on here'.

"Ms Stutz, could we get some preliminary information. Can you give us some statistics? What is your father's name?" When Fred interviewed witnesses or suspects he had a way of eliciting information from them that no other detective Oriole had known could do. He would sit in an interview and get confessions from suspects who were hardened by their experience.

"Daddy is Marvin Stutz.

"How long has your father lived in Prescott?"

"My Daddy moved here from Palm Springs three years ago to manage the Chino Pipe Line. After I graduated from ASU with my degree in accounting, Daddy offered me a job working in the office. I've been here two and a half years. I bought my condo two years ago." Fred and Oriole looked at each other and Fred raised his right eyebrow again in question.

"Ms Stutz, do you have a picture of your father?"

"A picture? Why do you need a photo of Daddy? What kind of a picture? How old? I don't understand. What is going on?" Marlene's rapid fire questions again raised concerns with the officers about her composure and honesty.

"Ms Stutz, we want a picture so we can make a comparison." Fred quietly responded.

"Well I have one from my brother's wedding last January. Would that work?"

"Yes, that's fine. Could you find it for us?"

Marlene tottered down the hall on her four inch heels and Fred whispered to Oriole, "A little nervous?"

"Ya think." Oriole whispered back. "Is she hiding something

or just her normal self?"

Marlene rejoined the detectives in a very short period of time. "Here. It's a duplicate you can just keep. Do you think you know something about where Daddy is? He just wouldn't not call me. He just wouldn't miss work. Something bad must have happened. I need to know. Can't you tell me what's going on?

"Ms Stutz, do you know if your father might have been involved in a relationship? Would he have gone off with someone without telling you?"

Marlene handed the picture to Oriole. In looking at the photo, she was 100% sure she had identified the dead body as Marvin Stutz. She nodded to Fred, who was in the process of assisting Marlene to be seated on the couch next to him.

"Ms Stutz, did your father have a habit of going off without letting someone know?" He reached out and touched Marlene's forearm.

"No, everyone loved Daddy." Oriole looked over Marlene's head at Fred and frowned a question.

"Did he carry large sums of money with him?"

"Oh, my God, he's been hurt, hasn't he. Where is he. I have to see him." Marlene's voice cracked and tears were marring her flawlessly applied makeup. The wadded up tissue she had been carrying was shredded in a pile on the Navajo rug. She folded over and went into hysterics.

"Ms Stutz, could you come down to the office with us to continue this interview?"

Oriole and Fred assisted Marlene into the back of the vehicle and drove to the Prescott office. At the office, Oriole had Marlene situated in a "soft interview room", a room they used to interview victims and kids. Oriole took the picture of Marvin Stutz to the ME for confirmation of identity. The ME concurred with Oriole that Marvin Stutz and the dead body were one in the same. They both agreed it wasn't necessary for Marlene to do the identification given the state of decomposition. Oriole met up with Fred and told him of the positive ID. Because of the rapport Fred had built with Marlene, Oriole suggested he handle the notification and the rest of the interview while she taped it and watched from the observation room.

Marlene's former hysterics were nothing compared to what

she displayed after Fred told her. She flung herself off the couch onto the floor, began screaming and crying, pounding the floor and kicking her feet. Oriole watched in amazement knowing that each person handled death differently, but thinking this was way over the top. Oriole listened as Fred went over many of the same questions again to make sure the answers were the same.

"Ms Stutz, I know this is difficult. I have just a few more questions if you could manage, then I'll have someone drive you home." Marlene crawled up the couch and made an effort to compose herself. "Ma'am, is there anyone who would want to harm your father?"

"No. No one. The only problem that ever existed is between Daddy and Jim. Daddy didn't think Jim was good enough for me. But it never came to blows or anything like that and anyway Jim has been in San Francisco at a conference for the last week. I just talked to him on his cell phone last night." She reined in her sobs and defiantly stuck out her chin. "Wait a minute. How did Daddy die? What happened? When?"

"Ms Stutz, it appears that your father died of gun shots. We don't have the exact time just yet."

"Did he kill himself? Not Daddy. Never. Oh, God, someone killed him didn't they. I knew it." Marlene started in with the hysterics again, much to Oriole's consternation.

"Ms Stutz, do you know how we can get ahold of Jim. What's Jim's full name and address?"

"It's James Worthington. I have his address and number in my PDA." Marlene began rummaging in her oversized Coach purse. "But he had nothing to do with this. He couldn't have, he's been gone all week."

Fred wrote down the information and nodded his head toward where he knew Oriole was listening and watching. Oriole had recorded the information and placed a call to the department secretary asking her to run his name.

After the interview with Marlene, Oriole and Fred accessed computer records on Marvin Stutz. The results were disappointing for information except for an injunction against harassment (IAH) filed in the Chino Valley Magistrate court by Stutz against Jim Worthington issued five months earlier. The IAH prohibited Worthington from being at the job site, Marvin's home and carrying firearms.

A follow up search on Worthington, turned up more tid bits: arrests for burglary, assault, forgery, and misconduct with a weapon. His last known address was out in Juniper Woods. Juniper Woods was a subdivision resulting from a massive division of an old homestead into five to forty acre mini ranches. Folks living in Juniper Woods hauled water, lived off the grid and tended to take care of their own problems. Most places had no trespassing signs accentuated with "property protected by .357" or similar identifiers. Those folks meant business.

Oriole and Fred decided to drive the thirty seven miles out to Juniper Woods to see if they could locate Worthington. They passed through Chino Valley, Paulden and proceeded out Highway 89. Off in the distance the San Francisco Peaks were visible through the light smoky haze from the latest forest fire. Antelope dotted the grassland, along with the occasional coyote.

They pulled off into the informal parking lot at the end of Bullock Road and reviewed the GPS directions to the last known address of Worthington. Directions took them down Bullock to Wapatee then to Side Saddle. They stopped a quarter of a mile before the identified property and got out the binoculars. The '60's trailer set back from the county road. The barbed wire fence surrounding the place was decorated with empty beer cans. The make shift gate was a steel post through four strand of barbed wire. A mean looking pit bull mix bared teeth and growled at their approach.

"How we gonna handle this?" Oriole whispered to Fred.

"We open that gate, we're trespassing."

"So let's just call him out." Ever practical, Oriole couldn't see going the hard way when an easy way seemed to present itself.

"Hello, the house." Fred yelled. And the dog started barking. The door to the trailer opened. A scrawny, bedraggled, shapeless woman appeared in the doorway.

"Whatcha want?"

"We're looking for Mr. Worthington. Is he here?" Fred shouted over the dog's noise.

"Who's asking?"

"I'm Detective Fred O'Neill, this is Detective Oriole Wolfe. We're from the Sheriff's Office. We need to talk to him."

"He won't be back til tonight. Whatcha want with Jim?"

"Business with him. Know where he is?" Fred decided his sentences could be just as short as hers.

"He went into town to get groceries. Why you want him?"

"Ma'am, what's your name?"

"Nunya."

"What, Nancy?" Fred knew what she meant, None Of Your Business. But he liked to jack hard asses around.

"None of your God damn business. Now get outta here."

Oriole and Fred returned to the 4 wheel drive SUV. "Let's go back to the office and get approval for a deputy to stake him out." Fred suggested to Oriole.

"Better yet, why don't we come back just about dusk and sit on the place."

"What if he slides in and we miss him? What if he has a Howitzer in there?"

"OK, let's make it around four o'clock. Surely, we'll be ahead of him. Why don't you drop me at the ranch and pick me up in a couple hours?"

Fred dropped Oriole off at Bear Ranch. No one was around, so Oriole went up to her room, changed clothes and went out to the barn. She opened the door to Buttercup's stall, the big buckskin she raised from a newborn foal. "Come on Buttercup, want to go for a ride to nowhere?" She saddled up, and headed out to the National Forest land that backed onto Bear Ranch. Oriole loved to ride and didn't have the opportunity to relax as often as she would have liked.

The ride was lazy, with Buttercup moving under her as if she knew exactly what Oriole needed. Teddy Roosevelt was quoted as having said there is something about the outside of a horse that's good for the inside of a man. Back then women weren't considered. But Oriole thought there was a lot of truth to the statement for women too. She rode off into the hills, watching the quail and their little babies, the occasional Road Runner, once in a while she'd spot a coyote. The time on Buttercup gave her an opportunity to let go of all the office stress, parenting frustrations, money problems and created a new woman. She turned Buttercup back to the ranch. As she rode into the corral, Summer walked out of the barn.

"Hey, girl, where you and Buttercup been?" As Summer stroked Buttercup's muzzle and blew into her nostrils.

"Summer, every time I'm on her, I give thanks to you for saving her for me. We went up Knob Hill and back around the wind mill. Absolutely perfect."

"Great, honey. Marlowe and Chalcey aren't back yet. Let's brush her down, and head up to the house. Are you going to be here for dinner or you gotta work?"

"I'll grab a bite, and Fred is going to pick me up. We get to do a stake out. Ugg. I might need some caffeine to take with."

"I have a pork roast that should be done and we can whip up a salad. You finish up and I'll get it on the table."

Oriole put her hand on Summer's arm and looked at her grandmother. "Summer, have I ever told you how much I love you and all you do for us?"

"Every day that little girl is here. See you in a few."

Summer went up to the house and made a pot of Jamaican Blue coffee and prepared sandwiches for Oriole and Fred.

Marlowe and Chalcey drove into the yard in Summer's 4-wheel drive pickup. Marlowe dropped Chalcey off at the barn to put away the poles and tackle, and walked into the house. "Hey, Summer look, we got supper. Cleaned and on ice." Summer looked at the cooler filled with limits of fresh fish.

"Sweeeet. How about dinner tomorrow for those little rascals? I got a roast going and Oriole has to leave soon."

"Work? That DB?"

"Yeah. Fred's picking her up. I made them some sandwiches and coffee cause they have a stake out."

Chalcey came in from the barn. "Summer, something's wrong with Puddles. Come quick, she's not moving." Marlowe, Oriole and Summer followed the fast moving Chalcey to the barn. Puddles, the rescued calico stray, lay on her side in the hay. When Puddles arrived, she was scrawny, infected with fleas and on her last legs. With the nurturing and medical treatment of Summer and the love and affection from Chalcey, she had flourished.

Summer knelt in the hay and examined Puddles. "Chalcey, I think she's gone."

"No." Chalcey cried scooping Puddles in her arms. "She can't be gone. I just fed her this morning." Her tears flowed. Body wrenching sobs followed. Oriole took Chalcey in her arms and held

19

her, soothing her with motherly comfort. Marlowe wrapped both of them in her arms. Summer got the shovel and a cardboard box and went out in the pasture and dug a hole.

"Chalcey, Puddles is gone. Let's make her a proper resting place and set her down. You go find some quartz for her head stone and some red agate to cover the grave. Do you want me to give the eulogy or can you do it?" Summer spoke to Chalcey very matter of factly, while inside she felt the pain and hurt Chalcey was exhibiting.

Between sobs Chalcey responded, "I'll try. If I can't, will you?"

"You bet."

Within the hour, the grave was dug, Puddles was placed in the box, and in the grave and red agate and quartz alerted anyone looking that here lay a special friend. After Chalcey gave the eulogy through sobs and tears, everyone trooped up to the house.

Afterward, Fred arrived in the yard. As he walked in the house, he could sense something was off with the four generations of women. "What's going on?"

"Shhh." Oriole put her finger to her lips. "Chalcey lost her cat today."

"Damn, which one? Not that little gray one?"

"No. Puddles, the calico."

"Oh, man that's hard. Where is she? Maybe Uncle Fred can make it better?"

"Chalcey, Uncle Fred's here. Do you want to come down and say hi?"

Chalcey heard Oriole and came downstairs, knowing that the teddy bear Fred would hold her and make her feel better.

"Hi, Fred. I lost Puddles today."

Fred sat down at the table and reached out his arms for Chalcey. "I know, honey. She was a good little friend, wasn't she? She followed you everywhere. When it's their time, they know and they don't want us to suffer for them. They were created to be friends to us and when they have done their job, they're called home. That's where Puddles is now. She's smiling down at you right now. She knows how your heart is breaking and she wants you to know she is fine. She wants you to mourn and remember the love she had for you. She'll be with you from time to time, you may even see her out of the corner of your eye, she might crawl up on your bed, and then one of these days another little Puddles will come to you. Puddles selected you out of all the people in the world to be with. Her spirit will be with you until you have reached resolution then surprise, surprise another will come along to replace her."

"Do you think that's really true or are you saying that to make me feel better?"

"Both, sweetie. Your heart is broken with her loss. Nothing right now will make you feel better. Soon, the heartbreak will turn to fond memories. And soon after that some other little creature will come into your life. Not to replace her and her memory, but to supplement. It's so we can learn how to love and how to let go. Until the time you are ready, she'll be with you. You'll feel her spirit. You'll see her in the barn from time to time. You'll talk to her. One day when you're ready, her spirit will bid you goodbye, and you watch, another little guy will come along."

"Did you see where we buried her? It's out there by that tree you got her from last summer." Chalcey's tears were still flowing, but the sobs had receded.

"Come and show me and we'll do another prayer for her, just you and me."

Chalcey took Fred out to the grave. Fred removed his Resistol cowboy hat and bowed while he prayed for Puddles' spirit. "Chalcey, I tell you what, let's make a collage of pictures you have of Puddles and I'll ask George to draw a water color of her and we'll put it in the hallway with all the other memories. How's that sound?"

"Yea, I think there are some on the computer. I can work on that tonight while you and Oriole are sitting in the dark."

Back at the house, Marlowe looked out the kitchen window, watching her granddaughter and the hulking detective. "Oriole, I didn't know Fred was so sensitive. Did this occur overnight, or have I been too busy to notice?"

"It isn't an overnight conversion. I've noticed it myself over the last few months. Actually, its been coming on since Marvelle passed. He seems more in tune with everything. I actually started liking him."

"They're on their way back. Let's put dinner on the table."

Summer and Marlowe set the table while Oriole gathered the makings for a tossed salad. By the time Fred and Chalcey walked in the door, food was on the table.

"Fred, I made sandwiches and coffee to go, but figured y'all might want to sit down to companionship before you had to leave for the fun." Summer explained the reason for the set table.

"Summer, I'm not one to ever turn down your vittles. And who knows when we'll return to the real world, we might starve to death without your help."

Marlowe watched the interaction between Fred and Chalcey over the simple supper and decided maybe Fred wasn't so bad after all.

As Fred had his second helping of meat and third helping of salad, he remarked, "Larapin, Summer, just larapin."

"What the hell is larapin, Uncle Fred?"

"Chalcey! You don't need to use that kind of language." Oriole scolded.

"Larapin means the grub is so good you can't find another word to express the tastes." Fred told Chalcey and looked over at Oriole to quiet her over protectiveness.

"Larapin. Larapin." Chalcey repeated several times to remember this new word. "Boy, Summer this roast is larapin."

The table dissolved into laughter. After they cleared the dishes, Fred and Oriole gathered their gear and extra provisions and left in the SUV.

On the way out to Juniper Woods, the partners kibitzed over Chalcey, Puddles and death that they dealt with daily. "You know, I'd forgotten just what tranquility exists on Bear Ranch until spending the time today with y'all. Maybe Chalcey and I can go riding tomorrow if we catch a break on the case."

"Fred, you don't even have to ask. You're always welcome. I know how much you miss Smoky and riding with Marvelle. Even if we're not around, you just grab a horse and tack and enjoy."

Discussion bounced around as only long time partners can do, until they arrived at the road a quarter of a mile from the trailer. Nothing was moving, no lights were on, and the old beater that had been in the yard was long gone. "Think she took a powder?" Oriole posited.

"Hard to say. She might have warned him and both high tailed it to nowhere. Let's just sit here and enjoy the afternoon, the breeze, the birds and we can pass the time playing I spy."

"Fred sometimes you're nuts." Oriole laughed at the crazy, but logical suggestion.

Close to dusk, they heard the rumble of pipes just before they saw the beater driven by the skanky broad, pull up to the locked gate. She unlocked the gate, drove the truck into the yard and pulled suitcases from the bed of the truck. From the ease with which she hefted them, Fred assumed the bags were empty. "Looks like she's getting ready to take a powder. Let's wait til she loads the truck and leaves. Then we can follow her or stop her."

"And just what is our probable cause to stop?"

"Well, now it could be the license plate light is burned out, or the pipes are too loud. Or maybe we won't stop her, but she'll have to stop because of our car." Fred was trying to find a legal reason to approach her.

"Let's just watch and wait for now and see what she's up to."

They didn't have to wait long. Skanky lugged two suitcases to the beater, got in and spun gravel leaving the yard. She didn't even bother locking the gate. Fred moved the SUV into the on coming path of the beater and locked up the brakes causing the beater to screech to a halt.

"What the hell's wrong with you?" Skanky yelled at Fred. "Get outta my way."

"Gee, ma'am I'm sorry." Fred cajoled as he exited the SUV. "I just need a minute of your time. Can you give that to me?" As he walked up to the driver's side, he could smell the unmistakable pungent aroma of marijuana emanating from the truck cab. While Fred was walking up to the truck, Oriole carefully pulled her duty weapon and held it just below the open window as she waited in the vehicle.

"Ma'am, y'all wouldn't have been smoking mary jane now would ya?"

"Get outta my way you stupid bastard. I got places to go, people to see, and things to do and you're holding me up."

"When I approached the vehicle to ascertain the safety and welfare of the driver who appeared to have lost control of the vehicle, I smelled an aroma coming from the cab, that based on my training and experience as a drug recognition expert, I determined to be Marijuana. Do you have a Medical Marijuana Card, Ma'am? No. Now little Missy, I can arrest you for being under the influence of a drug or metabolite, charge you with a bunch of felonies, or you and I can have a little chat and I might, I just might let you go on your way. What's it going to be?"

"Look, I know you want Jimmy. He's not here, hasn't been back, ain't coming back. I told him you were looking for him and he's lit out. Told me if I was smart so would I. I'm smart enough to know something's going on and I don't want any part of it. So, come on, let me get. I ain't done nothing to you." Skanky wheedled.

Oriole got quietly out of the car, carrying her gun down to her side and walked to the passenger side of the beater. "Are you Carla West?" Oriole had run the plate and it came back registered to Carla West.

"What if I am? You got no business with me." The skanky broad now had a name and had started crying.

"Carla, we need to talk to Jimmy. Where is he?" Oriole spoke softly, woman to woman. Fred and Oriole had done good cop bad cop so often whenever one started the other flipped roles.

"He told me not to tell. He said he'd give me a beating like he never had before and believe me he's done it a bunch." Her hands were shaking, snot was running down her nose and chin and where she had swiped at the mucus with the back of her hand, a trail of grime remained. "You don't know who you're dealing with, Jimmy, he's some kind of mean if you cross him."

"Carla, I can see that he's mistreated you. No one deserves that kind of abuse. Let me help you. I know women's shelters and counselors who can help you." Good cop Oriole continued building rapport with Carla.

Fred watched and waited while Oriole worked her magic on Carla, knowing sooner or later, they'd get what they were after.

"If I give you information, will you let me go?"

"Well, depends on what you can tell us." Oriole held Carla's attention.

"He said he was heading to Blythe. He's got family over there. He left about an hour after I called him when you were here before." She swiped again at her grimy face.

Fred and Oriole convened at the rear of the truck. "Should we cut her loose?" Fred whispered.

"Might as well. That girl is dumb as a box of rocks. I doubt we can get anything else from her. Let's find out where she's going though."

"Carla," Fred spoke again from the driver's side causing Carla to jump in her seat. "Where are you headed in case we need you again?"

"Look, I'm going home to my folks. They live down in the valley. I'll give you their phone number. They got my kids. They'll let me crash for a few days. They always know where I'm at." The sniveling slowed to a drip. Fred and Oriole took down the information and let her go. They took one last look around the un gated yard, couldn't locate the mutt, and decided there wasn't much of interest and left.

When they got back to the office, they called the Blythe police department to ask for a BOLO (Be On the Look Out), on Worthington and called it a day.

3

MONDAY MORNING, Summer had finished feeding the livestock and was having a cup of green tea in the kitchen when the phone rang.

"Summer, it's Richard Yellowhorse. How are you? I'm sorry to disturb you. I need to ask a favor. I need a sweat. Do you have time?

"Richard, you were with Oriole the other night, uh? Sure. How about tomorrow say 11:00."

"I gotta work tomorrow. Any way we can today?"

"Chalcey gets home about 3:30. Can you come at 1:00?

"I'll be there. Thanks.

Summer had been a practicing Shaman for over 20 years. Most of the Indians who needed help came to her because of her reputation and knowledge. She was trained as a Shaman by the Foundation for Shamanic Studies. Even though she was as White as they come, the Yavapai Apache, local Hopi and Navajo Native Americans respected her abilities.

Richard arrived on time, parked his truck in the driveway and saw that she had saddled two horses for the ride to the hogan she had built on the back of the ranch.

Summer had her bag ready and they mounted up and rode to the hogan together. "Richard, tell me what you have done so far."

"I called in my spirit guides to protect me. I was concerned his spirit might come back with me."

"Ok. I have everything ready at the hogan. I'll get it started and leave you to it. You've been here more than once."

They rode for about 30 minutes and arrived at the sweat lodge and hogan Summer had built for her indoctrination into Shamanic ways. She dismounted, tied Popeye to the rail and went into the lodge.

The sweat lodge was built in a circular dome, covered with hides, one of which served as the door. Summer had gathered the willow branches from the Verde River bed and dug the fire pit herself years ago. From the fire, she had taken the hot rocks and placed in the pit, along with sage and cedar for purification. Water was waiting in Hopi jugs next to the fire pit. Summer called in the spirits from the four directions and from Mother Earth and Father Sun. She asked the spirits to cleanse Yellowhorse from the death experience and then left the lodge to Richard.

"Summer, I'm home. Whose truck is that out there?" Chalcey was scrounging in the refrigerator as Summer walked into the kitchen.

"Chalcey, it's good to see you too. That's Richard Yellowhorse's truck."

"Where is he?"

"He's at the lodge."

"Oh. Why do they come to you for help? Don't they have their own Shaman?"

"Well, over the years the tribes around here have found I follow the traditional ways and they trust me. They know I'll treat them right."

"But why does Yellowhorse need a sweat?"

"Natives believe, and so do I, that if a spirit leaves its body unprepared, it wanders until it can find peace. Whenever Natives come upon a murder or violent death, they seek a sweat to purify and cleanse their soul and to help release the spirit of the deceased."

"Is that real?"

"Let me tell you about a time it happened to me. I had gone out with Oriole to a murder site. I could sense the spirit still there. I did a spirit release prayer. But when I got home, I discovered the spirit had come back with me. The young man's spirit wasn't ready to go home because he couldn't see home. He hung around for several days and I called the drummers to help me help him find his way across. I could tell right after that, he was at peace and home. That's one of the things that Yellowhorse didn't want to happen to him, that's why he did a sweat."

"Do we need to do a sweat for Puddles?" Chalcey, with all the seriousness of a 13 year old, asked her great-grandmother.

"Not a sweat. When we prayed over her, she knew where she needed to go."

"Do you believe Puddles had a spirit too?"

"Animals have spirits. They're different than yours and mine, but nonetheless they still have a spirit."

"So, if I see a dead person, I need a sweat?"

"You might need a sweat for other reasons too, like illness, emotional trauma, to pick a career, to make a big decision."

Chalcey chewed on that while eating her burrito. "I guess I'll wait on the sweat for awhile, cuz I'm not ready for a career, I'm not ill or emotionally traumatized, unless it'd be because I got too many mothers. The kids at school say I have three mothers."

Summer chuckled to herself and turned her back so Chalcey couldn't see the laughter in her face. "You got one mother—Oriole; one grandmother—Marlowe; one great-grandmother—me. Then you got lots of other relatives that are by heart if not by blood."

"Ok. I gotcha. I'm going to go for a ride with Red. I think I'll go up to Knob Hill. Is that OK?" Chalcey's independence was moderated by her common sense in letting people know where she was and what she was doing.

"It's nearly four. Be back in an hour so we can get supper on. Take the .22 just in case you come across rattlers. Take your cell too." If you lived on the ranch, you knew how to shoot and what to shoot at when necessary and even though Chalcey was 13 she had taken to shooting just like Oriole had.

4

MONDAYS CAME with law and motion day in Superior Court and juggling four different court rooms with 14 different clients, by noon, Marlowe wanted a cigarette and a Scotch, but she'd given up smoking and knew the Scotch would and could wait until she got back to the ranch.

The typical law and motion ran to pre-trial conferences for an alleged rapist, arsonist and meth head; initials on three new cases and the ordinary run of the mill clients who were in the wrong place at the wrong time with the wrong pants on. It seemed that whenever someone got caught with dope, the answer to the cops was, those aren't my pants, coat, shirt—someone must have put that in my pocket, purse, backpack.

And no matter how hectic law and motion day was, Marlowe loved it, the excitement, the challenge, the pain and the promise. Defense work was all she ever wanted from the time she entered law school commuting three days a week to Phoenix for four years while Summer looked after Oriole. The years had whizzed by as she built a reputation as a solid defense attorney in Coconino, Mohave and Yavapai Counties. Occasionally, Marlowe would take cases in Maricopa, La Paz or Gila County for friends or friends of friends, but on the whole the northern region was her comfort zone.

Corruption of the frontier days had been supplanted by strokes from good ole boys. Justice was still bought and sold, but with sophisticated barter and rewards of political reimbursements. And her goal was to challenge justice to overcome history.

Every day she saw the sign in the window of her downtown office, she smiled to herself. Marlowe Sharpe. Summer had named her after her late great grandfather, Marlowe Wilson. Sharpe came from the brief marriage to Johnston Sharpe, who died as a result of Hodgkin's disease before Oriole started school. The insurance policy covered law school and a college trust for Oriole. Almost as tall as Summer, with the same clear, ageless skin and blond highlights covering the advancing gray, she was as comfortable in a Carole Little or Jones New York suit as she was in blue jeans and Lucheses.

Marlowe had designed her office to fit her life style. The lobby was full of antiques collected from garage sales, auctions and second-hand stores. A drop down secretary desk hid office supplies, a wire meshed armoire held active files, and her secretary's desk consisted of file cabinets supporting a barn door that had been refinished by Marlowe herself. Since clients rarely lingered in the office, Marlowe had gone with simple but stout leather chairs rescued from an estate sale, between which sat an end table from her great-great-grandfather's ranch. The look and feel of country comfort continued into her office where instead of a desk she had a slab from a 250 year old alligator oak tree, cut and polished after it bit the dust in a huge wind storm some years back. Instead of client chairs, she had favored an old oak couch she found at a garage sale and had redone in dark mahogany brushed leather. Topping off the oak tongue-n-groove floor, she herself had done, was a Navajo rug given to her by friends of Summer's when she opened her doors to work. People who knew such things, often told her it was a mistake to use the rug, to walk on. It should be on the wall to admire. However, when Richard Yellowhorse's grandmother unrolled it in the office, she said, "this rug is to live on, walk on, learn on, and to soak up spirit." So, soak up spirit it has.

The first few years of practice the lobby had served as an after school hold over for Oriole, then one day, Joan walked in looking for a female attorney to handle a no contest divorce and she never left.

Joan's husband had skipped the country leaving her and her three kids without a pot to piss in or a window to throw it out. Joan Marshall's training was in corporate law, but she knew how to organize, manage and cajole attorneys to get done the daily necessities of a practice.

Marlowe didn't realize she needed a secretary until Joan took over the front office and the practice flourished. Potential clients would call in for a consult and Joan would screen them according to her own guidelines: serious—can pay; shopping—don't need the headache; desperate—they need us whether they can pay or not. And most of the ones who couldn't pay with money found other ways of paying for Marlowe's services—pigs, chickens, a horse now and then, hay, fencing, tractor work, plumbing and the new kitchen out at the ranch.

Joan would walk in to Marlowe's office and tell her "you need to help these people, they have a child that's a special needs and the school isn't following the IEP. I scheduled them in at 4:00 so you could talk with them. It just isn't right what that school is doing." And at 4:00 Marlowe would meet with the parents and take the case, money or no money.

Joan looked diminutive, but acted like a bulldog, 5' nothing, stylish clothes, that Marlowe helped her find at consignment stores, smoked like a stevedore, swore like a longshoreman and the biggest heart of anyone except perhaps Summer. Joan would help some of the unfortunate clients with a food basket or possible job, and others she'd give a kick in the ass and a kiss on the check.

Marlowe had helped set up a college fund for each of the Marshall kids from some of the child support Joan was awarded. As each one of the kids graduated from high school, Marlowe helped them get into college and oft times helped them stay there. Once the last one hit college, Joan decided she needed a hobby and took up square dancing for something to do. At 56, she looked more like 36, tight calf muscles, narrow waist, none of those saggy arms that come with age.

"Joan," Marlowe voiced louder than a conversation, but not quite a yell from her office, "what's the status of the motion to suppress on Calderon?"

"Listen, we had the intercom put in to save your voice. Just press the button and you speak normally." Joan had stepped into Marlowe's office door while chastising the misuse of the modern equipment.

"I just can't get used to it. I'll keep trying."

"The motion is hard copy on your desk, computer copy in the

folder for Calderon. I made some changes, just grammar. See what you think."

With Joan's experience and understanding, she could probably write the motion herself. Frequently, she drafted motions based on telephone conversations with Marlowe or clients and rarely did they require much perfection.

"The hearing is coming up, I really want to stick it to Arthur. He's such a prick. This is one of those that should never have been charged in the first place. No evidence, no witness, no crime. Bastard." Marlowe unloaded her disgust of Gentry Arthur, the assigned deputy county attorney. "The ass hole won't give me updated reports, disks, or photos and we're set for an evidentiary hearing and the judge won't continue. She says we'll hear what there is. How stupid is that?"

"All we need, Marlowe, is a blood expert to say it couldn'ta been Calderon and you got a defense verdict."

"Yea, but where can we find an expert for next to nothing who'll say there's no way it coulda been Calderon?"

"Ok, if we don't have money for an expert, we use the experts we got. Which officer do you know who knows more about blood spatter than any expert?"

"Great idea. There's that guy who's a former Seal. He's studied blood spatter, oh, and that guy from Mohave that has 35 years in as a federal agent. Can you get me one of them on the phone and let's see what they know." Marlowe started pacing her office.

5

ORIOLE AND FRED were pouring over the reports as Monday wound down into hum-drum grunt work. "Looks like Worthington played both women. We got CHPs, Blythe, DPS and the Mohave Sheriff on the alert for him. Wonder if Stutz knew about Skanky?" Fred was chuckling as he posed the question.

"Carla. Carla West."

"She'll always be Skanky to me. It's not my fault—I put a name on 'em and that's what sticks. I think we need to expand our horizons here, Oriole. We need to look at other options for Stutz's untimely death. Who else stood to benefit, who else did he cross, who else could be involved? Let's go in that direction while we wait to hear on Worthington."

"Ok, he was separated from his wife, who still lives over in California. Apparently, the will is the same one from years ago. All three inherit, wife and two kids. He had a life insurance policy for $250,000. Both kids were beneficiaries. In this report, it says Stutz was in business with some guy in Prescott Valley years ago, Bob Turnball. There is a note here they had a falling out. Doesn't say what about. Turnball is still in PV. So, we could divide and conquer. You take PV and daughter. I'll follow up on the phone with the son and wife. Let's meet back at the Ranch and I'll feed you so you don't have to eat any more of that garbage you call your home cooking. Say 6:30 for dinner. If you get done early, come on by and Chalcey can take you for a ride."

They separated the reports and worked their individual assignments. Oriole called Marlene to get her brother's phone number and address and asked about the wife/Marlene's mother's location. The information provided resulted in four phone calls to various parts to finally track down Jeremy Stutz, living in Tucson with his new bride.

"Mr. Stutz, this is Detective Wolfe, Yavapai County Sheriff's Office up in Prescott. Can I ask you some questions about your father?"

"I still can't believe it. I'm hoping I wake up and it was all a bad dream. But I guess that won't be happening, huh? Go ahead, what do you need to know about Dad?"

"First of all, my condolences. I know this is hard and certainly difficult for you over the phone. Are you going to be up here any time soon?"

"Jennifer and I will be up this weekend to help make arrangements. Do you want to meet then or talk now? Either way is OK with me."

"This weekend is fine. Can you tell me how to get ahold of your mother?"

"Oh, she and Dad have been separated for years. Gosh, maybe 15 years. She still lives over in Riverside. She's coming in this weekend too, even though they weren't together. They had a good relationship and remained friends. It's really been hard on everyone. Here's her number. You gonna call her or do you want to see all of us this weekend?"

"I'll call her now and plan on seeing her this weekend too. Can you think of anyone who would want to harm your father?"

"I've been thinking about that. I guess you do when there's a senseless death. Marlene's boyfriend of course rises to the top of the list. You know about the life insurance, but neither of us would harm Dad for anything. Mom gets everything else. Is it possible he was in the wrong place at the wrong time?"

"Jeremy, that's always a possibility." Oriole didn't say what was going through her head, always look at family first. "What time would you all be arriving on Saturday?"

"I'm picking Mom up in Phoenix about 10:00, so we should be in Prescott about noon. I'll call you when we get to the condo."

Oriole checked in with Fred and discovered he had pretty much struck out. She decided to work on some other open cases and let Stutz simmer until the weekend meeting.

Fred arrived at the Ranch about 5:30 to the delight of Chalcey. "Mom said you'd be coming for dinner, but she said you and I might go for a ride together. Can we?"

"If you're waiting on me, you're backing up. Come on. I hear you got a special place up on Knob Hill to show me." They saddled up, her on Red and Fred on Popeye. The ride was slow and easy and Fred talked about family, life, and what Chalcey was doing in school. They returned just in time to brush down the horses, feed the critters and get washed up for supper.

Marlowe arrived home in time to see Fred and Chalcey return from their ride. As she watched Fred and her granddaughter cross the yard to the backdoor, she was again awed by his compassion and genuine caring for Chalcey. She reflected on this man she had known for many years in a new light.

6

"DETECTIVE WOLFE, this is Jeremy. We are about 20 minutes out of Prescott. We can meet you at Marlene's. We've been talking on the way up and Mom seems to think there might be some stuff you need to know."

"I'll call Detective O'Neill and have him join me. See you soon."

Oriole speed dialed Fred, "Fred, the family will be here in 20 minutes. I'll swing by your place and pick you up."

Oriole and Fred stood on the door step of the condo, preparing for the unpleasant task, "Our condolences to all of you during this tragedy." Fred began. "We know you have a lot to do to take care of business, so we'll try to be brief."

"Mrs. Stutz, you indicated you might have some information that could be helpful. Could you tell us about that?" Oriole followed up with her earlier phone call to Mary and Jeremy.

"Please let's all sit down. Would you like something to drink?" Mary Stutz had taken over the role of hostess for her daughter. It was obvious looking at Mary that she was the one in charge. Standing a couple inches taller than Marlene, with blonde perfectly coiffed hair, in a Prada suit, Jimmy Choo shoes and enough bling to light up the house at Christmas time, Mary was a woman to be reckoned with. Just ask her, she'd tell you. Fred looked at her right hand as the sun caught the sparkle from the Red Diamond 2 carat ring. Fred thought, shiny as a new dime in a goat's ass.

"No thanks, we're fine."

"Well, you know Marvin and I separated years ago, but have remained, I mean had remained good friends. I wanted to pursue a career and he helped me get through college while the kids were young. He needed some financial help a few years back and I loaned him some money. Marvin had several corporations and two business partners; I have the names, phone numbers, that sort of thing. But what you really need to understand is why we separated. I believe that may have something to do with Marvin's death. The kids know, but no one else knows. It's been our family secret. I know nothing is sacred where murder is involved but if you can honor our request to keep a low profile on this it would help all of us." Mary looked at her two children who nodded agreement.

"Ma'am, you'll have to give us more information." Fred prodded Mary.

"Back when we got married, what 30 years ago, there was only one thing to do and that was get married and have kids. Look how things have changed, Marlene has her career and Jeremy waited until this year to marry. Marvin and I had been friends from the time we were 9 and 11. We were a couple in high school; the only choice we had was to get married when he finished college. I could sense a lack of–oh I don't know I guess a lack of commitment on Marvin's part. It was like he was missing out on something. He never held it against us. He just wasn't completely happy."

Oriole stole a glance at Fred, Fred raised his signature eyebrow like here it comes.

Mary had worked up the courage and dove in, "You see, Marvin, well, He was a good man."

"Mom, just spit it out," Jeremy almost yelled. "Or I will."

Oriole was thinking, someone better spit it out or I'll lose what's left of my sanity.

Mary began to pace on the Navajo rug, wringing her hands and creating an atmosphere of anxiety. "Ok alright, let me do it. Marvin was interested in alternative life styles."

"What do you mean alternative life styles, Mrs. Stutz?" Fred was as confused as a bee that'd been sprayed with bug spray and hadn't quite given up the ghost.

"Why, you know, he was gay." The condemnation oozed from Mary's bright red lips.

"Mrs. Stutz, there are lots of gay and lesbian folk around here. What did that have to do with Mr. Stutz's death?" Oriole felt her teeth grind in frustration.

"Why, there are people out there who kill gay men. That's what happened. Marvin went somewhere and someone found out and killed him."

"Mrs. Stutz, who found out. Where did Mr. Stutz go?" The last 20 minutes had been spent listening to this self-righteous homophobe and they were no closer to information about Marvin Stutz's death.

"Mrs. Stutz, why don't you go with my partner, and I'll talk to Jeremy, Marlene and Jennifer." Fred and Oriole separated the family. Oriole got stuck with Mary because Fred was known to have educated homophobes a little too severely because firsthand experience in his family had created sensitivity in him.

Mary and Oriole went into Marlene's home office, while the kids and Fred remained in the over white living room. "Jeremy, what can you tell me? Is there an angle here we need to know about?"

"No. Mom's never came to grips with Dad's life style. If Dad got the flu, it was cause he was gay, if his truck broke down, it was cause he was gay. She's just over the top on this. Dad never flaunted it. He wasn't swishy. None of the guys on the pipeline knew. None of his partners knew. He told me when I started college because he felt I could handle it by then. I told Marlene so she wouldn't be blown away. Dad was a great guy. His being gay didn't have anything to do with his death."

"Did he have a particular friend? Did he hang out at gay bars?"

"You'll have to ask Marlene. I've only been up here a couple times since they moved to Prescott. I don't know much about Dad's private life here." Jeremy and Jennifer sat together holding hands. They were close to a perfect match. Jeremy had almost white blond hair, unwavering blue eyes. He wasn't much taller than Jennifer, who was petite, blond and seemed so sweet, butter wouldn't melt in her mouth.

Marlene added, "No gay bars. Dad did talk about this one friend, Gary something. They met at a benefit at Sharlot Hall Museum and caught a couple movies, but it wasn't a serious relationship. Dad was pretty much a loner." Rivulets formed as tears began to fall. "But you need to know something, Mom doesn't know yet, neither does Jeremy. See, Dad felt it was time to cut the strings and get a divorce. I don't think anyone else knew. Dad sure hadn't told Mom. He was waiting for the right moment. It just never came."

In the office, Oriole was making small talk with Mary to get her to settle down. "Mrs. Stutz, when was the last time you spoke to or saw your husband?"

"Well, we were friends, but we hardly kept in daily contact, you know. I guess the last time was back when Jeremy and Jennifer got married. But I did keep in touch with emails. We still had business together and we had the kids."

"When were the last emails?"

"Well, I got an email a couple of weeks ago, I guess. It was brief, just an update on the Pipe Line, the weather, Marlene, what Marvin had been doing, that kind of thing. Nothing out of the ordinary." The rendition seemed too pat, too rehearsed for Oriole's comfort.

"Will you excuse me for a moment, I need to talk to my partner."

Oriole walked down the hall and made eye contact with Fred, nodded toward the kitchen for him to join her.

"What have you found out, anything good?" Fred asked.

"She seems to be reciting a prepared speech. Anything from the kids?"

"He was planning a divorce."

"Get outta here. Mary never mentioned it. Don't you think that's important? Why wouldn't she bring it up?"

"Marlene says she didn't know. I find that real hard to believe. Let's switch places and you work on the business aspect and I'll take on Mary."

Partners switched rooms and took the combined knowledge to dig for more information.

"Mrs. Stutz, tell me what you know about Marvin's last days?" Fred quietly entered his interrogation mode.

"Well, I already told Detective Wolfe everything. Why don't you talk to her?" Mary snippily responded.

"Mrs. Stutz, I spoke to Jeremy and Marlene, then I spoke to Detective Wolfe. There might be information you can add. When was the last time you heard from Marvin?" Fred patiently inquired.

"We didn't talk much anymore. He had his life and I had mine. We kept in touch by email."

"What was his frame of mind the last time you heard from him?"

"He was fine. He was working hard, long hours, but that was normal. He wanted us all to get together soon."

"Did he say why he wanted to get the family together?"

"He said he had some things to discuss, business things to update. I suppose he wanted to see all of us together." Mary evasively responded.

"Did he give you an idea of what he wanted to discuss about business or personal stuff?" Fred kept prodding.

"He said he had told Marlene and was going to tell Jeremy."

"Did he tell you? Did Marlene tell you?"

"Ok, OK, OK. He said he wanted a divorce. Are you happy now?" Mary's voice had reached a screech.

"Did he say why he wanted the divorce?"

"Can't you just leave it alone? He's dead and there won't be a divorce. It's not something we need to get into." While her voice had returned to normal levels, the force with which she spoke indicated she was still angry.

"What would the divorce have meant to you, to the kids?" Fred continued trying to elicit information.

"Nothing. Absolutely nothing. Nothing would have changed. It wasn't going to happen. I would never give him a divorce and he knew it. I don't believe in divorce. He has asked before and the answer is always the same. No, no, no. He said he wanted to move on with his life." Mary started to tear up and she reached for tissue to blot her eyes to avoid messing her makeup.

"So, he seemed anxious to get on with his life. Did he mention why now?" Fred paraphrased and extrapolated.

"He said he'd met someone. Can you believe it?" Mary was openly sobbing now. "I gave him the best 30 years of my life and he wanted out, wanted someone else. He wanted a man. I could have understood if it was another woman. But he wanted another man. I wasn't going to be the laughing stock of all my friends. Thrown away for a man." In between sobs, spittle erupted from her mouth onto Fred.

Fred wiped his arm where it landed and kept on. "Did he say who the other man was?"

"I told him I didn't want to hear about it. I didn't want to know his dirty little secrets. Then he emailed me that he was going to file the first of next month. That it didn't matter anymore. He said he had a right to be happy with his new love. New love. I wanted to puke."

"Did he say who his new friend was?"

"He said he had met him up here. He didn't say who. How could he do that to me, to us? I would never be able to look my friends in the eye again. How completely selfish. How unfair to me." She slapped the desk with such force the pencil holder bounced.

Fred decided to make hay while he could. "I can understand your frustration. Did the two of you talk about this or just email?"

"I couldn't talk to him. Whenever he'd call and I knew it was him, I wouldn't answer. That's why he emailed me. He seemed to think if he had news everyone wanted to hear it and that's just not right. I was so mad at him." If her anger now was any measure when he emailed her, she had been truly pissed off.

"Do you still have the email he sent you? It might help us."

"What? Why would I keep the email? To look at and hurt. I deleted it immediately. I didn't want anything to remind me of the hurt."

Fred decided he gleaned as much as he was going to for the time being and suggested they rejoin Oriole and the kids.

"I think we're about done here," Fred stated, "if we have further questions we'll call. If you can think of anything else, please don't hesitate to call either one of us. Thanks for your time." Fred and Oriole returned to the SUV and the office in Prescott.

"Seems to me Mary just rose to the top of the list. We need to go out to the Pipe Line and interview the employees out there. Let's see if we have enough for a warrant on the computers to verify the emails. If we split these up maybe early next week we can go out to Chino." Fred was dishing out assignments.

7

ON MONDAY, Oriole contacted the on-duty deputy county attorney to discuss a warrant and was told at this time there wasn't enough to issue a warrant. She contacted Marlene out at the offices and made an appointment for 1:30. Fred had already checked Mary's whereabouts for the week prior to Marvin's disappearance and it appeared she was able to account for her time.

Fred and Oriole drove out to the Pipe Line offices north of Paulden. The offices consisted of a construction trailer equipped with electricity and water, sitting in the middle of big rigs waiting to be put to work digging, moving, hauling and compacting earth. The steps up to the office were metal, make shift, a little rickety and unsecured. Inside, Fred and Oriole found Marlene, and three other people waiting.

"Detectives, this is Janelle Jankowski our office manager, Steven Smith our field supervisor, and Mark Littleton our crew chief. This is Detective Fred O'Neill and Detective Oriole Wolfe. They're here to ask some questions about Marvin and whatever they need we will provide it. Any questions?" Marlene had seemed rather diminutive in previous interviews, but here she was in her element, ordering people around, taking control. The three were a motley crew.

Fred looked at Oriole as if to say how do you want to do this, and immediately she began to provide the purpose of the investigation.

"Thank you, Ms. Stutz. We're here to gather background information about Mr. Stutz. Are there a couple offices we can use that will be out of your way?"

"You can use mine and Marvin's, just down this hall. I'm not planning on getting any work done anyway."

The office on the left reflected a female hand, a vase of dried silk flowers, a framed poster on the larger wall, and a diffuser on the metal desk. Obviously, Marlene's office. Oriole indicated she would take it. Fred and Marlene moved across the hall to the other office. Marvin's identity was evident with trade magazines, blue prints, and an old style horse shoe hat rack.

"Oriole, you take Janelle and I'll start with Mark. Marlene would you show them in please."

Janelle seemed over-dressed and out of place on a construction site. Janelle Jankowski's physical attributes preceded her. Long blonde tresses bounced on her shoulders as she entered the office on stiletto heels as out of place in a site office as a ball gown at a picnic. Her makeup was expertly applied to emphasize her best features and minimize less attractive gifts. The above the knee skirt split up the back for walking ease, revealed shapely legs accustomed to admiration. Finishing her professional attire was a cotton knit top purchased for a 34B accommodating a 34E. Oriole seated herself behind Marlene's desk and profiled Janelle as a former Las Vegas/Laughlin show girl, without the benefit of education as to proper construction attire.

"Ms Jankowski, please be seated. Can I get some basic information about you? Full name, address, date of birth?"

"Yeah, sure. Whatever you need." Janelle provided all that Oriole asked for.

"How long have you worked here? And where did you work previously?"

"I got hired here about 10 months ago as a file clerk then the office manager left 'cause she was pregnant and I took over as office manager about five months ago."

Oriole didn't miss the fact that Janelle had failed to provide previous employment. "And prior to this?"

"Why do you need that? My previous work history isn't pertinent to this job." Janelle became defensive.

"If it's not pertinent, there is no reason not to provide it.

Right?" Oriole had been a good student to Fred in how to turn the interview around.

"Well, I worked in Las Vegas and Laughlin at the casinos. Satisfied?"

Oriole kept at it, "Doing?"

"I was in the chorus line, OK. I don't see what that has to do with this." Miffed, Janelle shifted in her chair.

"How did you get the job here?"

"Like most people, I applied for it. A friend mentioned there was an opening and I was ready to move on and this seemed like as good a place as any. I sent in my resume and Marlene called me for an interview. I started the next week. Been here ever since. OK?" Anger was replaced by condescension.

"How well did you know Marvin Stutz?"

"Not too well at first, then after I got the office manager, we had daily contact. He was a nice guy, a truly nice guy. He told me what my job was, showed me what he wanted and let me do it. Once in awhile, we'd grab lunch or a drink, but other than that I didn't see him but briefly. I don't think Marlene liked having me around though. I think she was jealous of me. The guys on the job would work to find a reason to come into the office when I first started. Then it wore off. But I don't think she liked it. She was real territorial about Marvin and that no good boyfriend of hers. As if!" Janelle had warmed to the subject.

"Did Marvin have problems with anyone?" Oriole knew about Jim but wanted to see if it was common knowledge and if there was anything else going on at the job site.

"Well, Jim of course, they got into a shouting match about three months ago and Marvin gave him the boot." Janelle leaned closer and looked conspiratorially over her shoulder, then continued. "No one knows but Steven and Marvin were at each other's throats. I think Steven's time was limited." Satisfying herself with divulging a major secret, Janelle leaned back, crossed her legs and inspected her artificial nails.

"Anything else you can think of that might help?" Oriole didn't give the satisfaction that Janelle had sought, but glossed over the revelation.

"No, nothing else." Now Janelle was sullen and ready to terminate the interview.

"Thanks for your cooperation. If you think of anything else, call us please." Oriole walked her to the doorway, ready to glean information from the next person, but first she wanted to meet with Fred.

"Mark, can I get some information on you, full name, etc.?" Fred had taken Marvin's office to meet with the crew chief.

"Sure." Mark Littleton seemed at home in the work trailer. His blue jeans and work shirt were dusty and a little frayed. His boots were covered in mud. He appeared at ease with the detective as the interview began.

"It's so sad about Mr. Stutz. He was a great guy and a terrific boss. He recognized a good job and rewarded it. I started out on the line and I was eager to learn and he let me. This job opened up when Roberto returned to Texas and I asked if he thought I was ready. He said, 'you know as much about it as anyone else, let's put you in as interim and see.' That was five months ago and he made me crew chief in two months. He was a great guy. All the guys say so, well, there's one or two who hold a grudge, but except for them."

"Any of those guys have it in for Mr. Stutz?"

"No, not really. Jim's gone, Bill's here, but has cooled down. There might be a problem though with the super. See, we've been here almost three years and we've inherited guys from other projects as they close down. That's how we got Bill and Steven. Oh, and it has to be SteveN, not Steve. Just so you don't make that mistake. Bill came from Wyoming and Steven, I think, came from California. There were some hard feelings all the way around when we had to take them on, especially guys resented Steven. They felt he wasn't good enough to be a super and I think Mr. Stutz was in their corner. Marvin rode him pretty hard, but he had to otherwise the job wouldn't get done."

"Did SteveN do anything, say anything that might have led you to think he would harm Mr. Stutz?" Fred could sense there was more information just waiting to be pulled.

"Well, I probably shouldn't be talking out of school here, but Steven has a past and Marvin found out and was worried he might be continuing. Not that I would know of course. But there's talk. "

"What kind of a past?" Fred could see a downhill snowball picking up momentum.

"You just look at Steven and you can see what kind of past.

Look at those tats. He's done time. I don't even think his real name is Smith. Who uses Smith or Jones, except guys who don't want their real past to surface." When Mark finished it was with a simper. Fred had to look to make sure the complainer hadn't been replaced by a junior high girl.

"Anything else you can think of that might help us?"

"Not that I can think of."

"Thanks for your time. I'll walk you out." Fred wanted to get to Steven, but first wanted to compare notes with Oriole.

As Fred stood in the doorway of Marvin's office, Oriole came back down the hall. Fred nodded to her to join him as he backed into the office and she shut the door.

"Good stuff?" Oriole inquired.

"Maybe. How'd you do with Legs?"

"Legs? Oh, Janelle. She thinks there might be something with the super."

"Hmmm. So does Mark. Let's see if we can get prints on Smith. See if you can find a glass or soda."

Oriole went in search of cokes as Fred went out to the front office to find Steven. Steven Smith presented as burly, surly, and moved with a swagger. Not at all what you'd expect as a construction supervisor. His long sleeve shirt covered any arm tats, but the neck tats showed. Fred's experience with prison tattoos told him Mark's assessment was probably on target.

"Mr. Smith, I appreciate your time. Detective Wolfe is scaring up some cokes. Care for one? Can we start with some background information? Full name, date of birth, address." Fred knew Smith would be on guard if he was what he appeared to be.

"I'm not thirsty. Thanks anyway. I got work to do. Let's get this over with so I can get back to it." He slouched in the chair in front of the desk, jutted out his chin and lit up a cigarette as he provided the background information Fred sought.

Oriole returned with two cokes and a diet coke and set them down on the desk in front of Fred and Smith. She moved to the side of the desk and leaned on the computer stand, opening the diet coke. Fred took one of the cokes, drank long, smacking his lips, before setting it down in front of him. Smith reached out for the other popped the top and began drinking.

46

"So, Mr. Smith, can I call you Steven? How long have you been with the company?" Fred wanted to get more information about this unlikely supervisor.

"Been here for about five months. With the pipeline about two years. Transferred in from California after we finished up over there."

"How well did you know Mr. Stutz?"

"Didn't socialize if that's what you're asking? Saw him every day, talked to him about progress and problems. He did his job and I did mine. And damn well. I don't care what anyone else says."

Fred listened as Smith finished, but wasn't sure if Smith meant he did a fine job or Stutz did. "Did Stutz have any issues with any of the guys around here?"

"He was a nosy nell about everything. Had to know what they were doing on and off the job. I told him to butt out, but he said it was his job to make sure that the guys were clean and sober, on and off time. Wanted piss tests. I told him that was crazy, so what if they do a little this and that off hours. No skin off his nose. But he kept pushing. These guys work hard and play hard. I told him to mind his own business and leave my guys alone. It almost came to blows." Smith was working up to an attitude.

"That must have been difficult for you, having someone try to interfere with your crews like that." Fred empathized with Smith to elicit more information and drank down his coke, while Oriole was taking notes.

"You have no idea. But I made him understand what his job was and what mine was. He didn't like it. What was he gonna do? He didn't have any balls."

Oriole stole a glance at Fred as she continued to record her notes. "Did Mr. Stutz ever say anything about that?"

"Of course not, there was nothing he could say. When all that started I told him to tread lightly, that we were a long ways from the main office and to leave me alone. He knew he wasn't really my boss. I tolerated him for appearance sake and that was it."

"Did you and him ever have more than words?" Fred wanted to see just how deep a hole Smith would dig.

"Nah, he was a light weight. He just talked a lot."

"Mr. Smith, what are your plans now?" Oriole, anxious to get out of there and back to the sheriff's office, tried to move the interview along.

"Same ole, same ole. They'll send out a new project manager, who can read plans, do cost overruns and smooze politicians. I'll keep doing what I do. Are we about done here? I need to get out to the line." Smith stood to leave.

Fred and Oriole shook his hand. Smith threw the coke can in the garbage and left. Oriole closed the door while Fred pulled out a glove and grabbed the coke can. Oriole handed him an evidence bag he marked and sealed. They took their leave of Marlene and Janelle.

After returning to the office, Oriole left the evidence bag with the technician to lift and process the prints, hoping to identify Smith. Oriole suggested Fred come out to the ranch for supper and left for home.

8

MARLOWE FINISHED UP a motion to suppress evidence, put it on Joan's desk and called to see if Summer needed anything from town before heading out.

Joan finished up the stuff in her in box and left early for her square dance class. Marlowe looked out the windows onto the street and pondered how much Prescott had grown in the last 20 years. She considered opening the cabinet and pouring a drink, but rejected the idea because of the crack down on drinking and driving, and also because the cops would dearly love to pull her over and haul her off to jail. Gathering up her briefcase and several legal journals, she turned out the lights, locked the door and drove home.

Sitting in the driveway was Fred's truck. Marlowe felt a surge of excitement at the thought of seeing him and didn't quite understand the emotion. It had been years since she allowed personal needs or feelings to surface, raising Oriole, helping with Chalcey, working the ranch, it had all taken its toll on time and energy. In the last few weeks, seeing Fred hang out with Chalcey and Oriole had opened new vistas for Marlowe in terms of life. Marlowe walked up the steps to the large wraparound porch to find Summer sitting in one of the four rocking chairs.

"Fred's here again? Fancy that." Marlowe greeted the family matriarch.

"He seems to be blending in here. Part of that has to be due to Marvelle's passing even though she has been gone for over a year, but part of that has to be cause he is comfortable with us. Chalcey likes him, he cares about her, he's a good influence on her. Not to mention how well he and Oriole work together. He brought us a salmon for dinner tonight. Haven't had salmon in a long time. Dinner in 30 minutes. Everybody's out at the barn. Why don't you run up and change, I'll fix a drink and you go out to check on progress with the critters." Summer was encouraging Marlowe to get in the middle of the activity with Fred.

Oriole and Chalcey watched Fred work Red in the round pen, using a longe rope. "Why does Fred run him in a circle like that?" Chalcey's curiosity overcame politeness.

"He's teaching Red some manners. Horses are like kids they need to be reminded of how they are supposed to act." Marlowe had joined the two younger generations at the rails.

"Marlowe!" Chalcey jumped down from her perch to join her grandmother and put her arms around her squeezing tight. "We get salmon tonight. Fred's staying for supper and then maybe do you think we can all go for a ride?"

Marlowe looked over at her daughter for agreement, then out in the round pen, but Fred was busy working Red. "We'll see Chalcey. Are the animals fed?"

"Every one of them but Red. We can't feed him if he's going to work. We have to brush him down then put out his Timothy hay. See I remember." Chalcey proudly recited the proper procedures for her horse.

"Looks like Red is just about to graduate. Let's get his stuff ready, brush him down, don't feed him just yet. Let him settle down first. Then we'll see about a ride depending on everybody's schedule. I'm going up to help Summer with supper. Be sure and put everything away when you're done." Marlowe climbed down from the rails and walked to the kitchen.

"Summer, how's about I make that Caesar salad for supper? I can set the table if you like. If we use every day stuff, it can go in the dishwasher and maybe we can all go on a ride after dinner." Marlowe's offer was double pronged.

"We got four horses and five people, Marlowe. Who gets left behind?"

"We could get John's Appy. He always said anytime we wanted to, we could ride. Then we'd have enough. When's the last time you been out? It'd be good for you too." Marlowe was scheming and knew Summer knew it.

During supper, talk centered on Red's progress, the after dinner ride, Chalcey's school work. Obvious avoidance of Fred and Oriole's cases and Marlowe's clients didn't dampen the mood. Marlowe and Summer cleaned up the kitchen while everybody else saddled up.

John rode his Appy over and drove Summer's truck back home. The five of them left the ranch in single file, following the trail up Knob Hill onto the forest land. The ranch was positioned perfectly for unlimited access to countless acres of government land.

Chalcey and Oriole moved in beside Summer, while Marlowe and Fred lagged behind.

Fred worked at small talk until the party made the loop back to the ranch. "There's a new movie out, been out about a week. I hear it's supposed to be pretty good." The normally composed, fearless detective found himself flummoxed.

"What's it about?" Marlowe had to smile to herself at his lack of composure.

"It's a western. Think you might want to see it?" Sweat broke out on his forehead.

"Fred O'Neill. Are you asking me out on a date?" Marlowe had been jockeying for closer contact with Fred and was enjoying his predicament too much to just say yes.

"Well, not a date. I mean we could just see a movie. You know. You don't have to label it a date. I mean what if we did go on a date and you found out I stunk. I don't mean stunk like stink. I mean like you didn't like me. Then where would we be and would I be cut off from Chalcey. So, no not a date. Just a movie. Just to do something adult like. Not adult movie. I mean you know just without kids. Oh, shit, Marlowe do you want to go to the movie or not?" Fred's size 10.5 couldn't fit any further down his throat.

Marlowe rode on ahead to keep Fred from seeing her laughter. "So, this isn't a real date. It's just friends going to a movie cause neither of us has anything better to do? Right?"

Fred felt himself getting in deeper in the quagmire of this relationship stuff. "Oh, forget it. I should never have brought it up.

It wasn't a good idea. You know I just figured we've known each other for 20 years, what harm could there be. Well, that's not what I meant. I mean we're into the same things, same philosophy, even though you bust them out when I put them in. But, oh, never mind. Just never mind."

"Fred, I'd love to take in a movie with you. When?" Her capitulation came as a surprise to him while he was still in the process of pulling his foot out of his mouth.

"When. You said when. You really want to go. You know we don't have to go to a movie, I mean we could go anywhere, dinner, or 4 wheeling or on a ride. I mean whatever." Fred tried to shut his mouth to keep quiet, but the words kept tumbling over his former silver tongue.

That evening after Fred left the four generations were discussing the day's events and Marlowe let drop that she was going to the movies Saturday.

Oriole sing-songed, "Marlowe's got a date, Marlowe's got a date."

"Can I come too?" Chalcey asked, unfamiliar with any of the women in her life actually having a date.

"No, sweetie. We'll do something else." Summer suggested in an effort to divert Chalcey.

"What? I haven't been to a movie in forever. I never get to do anything fun."

"Chalcey, enough." Oriole's motherly reaction left no doubt Chalcey was not to continue.

"What say you and Oriole and I go to the zoo?" Summer suggested.

"How about Out of Africa instead?" Chalcey had cheered up.

"Oriole whadda you think?" Summer decided she might need to get an OK from her granddaughter for the excursion.

"Ok. On one condition. I get to drive and we get to stop for dinner at Antigua Cantina." Oriole knew if left to Chalcey lunch would be some fast food place.

9

ORIOLE AND FRED CHECKED IN with the fingerprint tech for progress of the real Mr. Smith to discover Mr. Smith was actually Stephen Walsh, formerly a guest at the California State Prison system and points east. Charges ranged from burglary to drugs. It seemed worth another trip to Paulden to inquire of Mr. Smith/ Walsh and his change of name.

"Mark, I'm warning you, you need to stay out of it." Janelle Jankowski implored the crew chief over lunch in the employee trailer.

"Butt out Janelle. You don't know what you're talking about. Everybody has stood by and been raked over the coals by Stutz and now by Smith, who thinks he's going to take over. Just leave it be." Angrily, Mark shot back.

The door opened and Marlene walked in followed immediately by Smith. "The detectives are on their way out to get some more information. I need you all to stick around." The authority with which Marlene delivered the order was not well received by any of the three listeners.

"Well, they can just come find me, I got work to do." Smith retorted.

"Marlene, it's time to get something through to you, you ain't the boss. Your daddy was project manager and you're nothing but the accountant. So, don't go acting like some high and mighty control freak." Mark pointed a finger at Marlene while moving toward the trailer door.

Smith hurried out to his truck, picked up a duffel bag from the front seat and moved it to the locked tool box in the bed of the truck, then left for the job site half a mile away. Oriole and Fred arrived to see his dust settle.

"Marlene, how are things going?" Fred greeted the discombobulated daughter of the deceased.

"I'm thinking about moving on. Maybe Tucson or Riverside. I don't much like it here anymore without Dad." Tears formed as she spoke.

"I'm so sorry to hear that. Has something happened?" Oriole comforted Marlene.

"Everybody is so rude and mean. I only took this job to be close to Dad. I can get a job with any of the accounting firms. There's nothing to keep me here now. I just can't stand it." Her voice rose with emotion.

Fred and Oriole looked at each other for a moment. "Detective Wolfe, why don't you talk to Marlene and Janelle and I'll talk to Smith and Littleton?" Fred suggested by way of escaping Marlene's whining. He took off to the job site after being told where Smith and Littleton most likely were, leaving Oriole to deal with the office staff.

Fred could see the two men toe to toe next to Littleton's truck engaged in a heated argument. He was pretty sure Smith would come out on top regardless of what the argument was about, based on sheer size and attitude. "Gentlemen, just the two I'm looking for. I have a few more questions. Could I impose on you to help me with some more information?" Fred used his most diplomatic tone.

"What the fuck do you want now?" Smith all but yelled.

"Actually, I'm here to see you, Mr. Walsh."

Smith's face turned red and he stiffened. Littleton took a step back to get out of harm's way. "My name is Smith. I dropped Walsh years ago. I got the paper work to make it legal. So, bite me." Mr. Attitude sneered at Fred.

"Why didn't you tell us that yesterday when we were here? It makes it look real suspicious, know what I mean?

"Cause it's none of yer business. I did my time. You got no reason to hassle me." Littleton faded back into the scenery as

Smith/Walsh argued with Fred.

"We just want to know why you lied to us that's all. Put yourself in my shoes. If someone lies to you, don't you want to know why?"

"Listen, I'm clean, I got nothing to hide. I just don't like cops. Now leave me alone I got work to do, mine and Stutz's." Smith/Walsh started walking off and Fred let him go knowing he could get to him whenever he wanted. Returning to the office trailer, he found Oriole stepping down the rickety stairs.

"Get anything from him?" Oriole greeted Fred.

"Makes me suspicious. Mr. Attitude's hiding something even though he was quick to tell me he wasn't. Let's go back to the office, I've got some ideas to follow up on and we've got a new case to start."

"Another DB?"

"Naw, just fraud. No blood and guts. Just heartache and headaches." Fred hated fraud scheme cases more than he hated doing dishes and he stocked his house with paper plates.

Waiting for them back at the sheriff's office was Joe Best from the Phoenix DEA office. In the past, the three had worked a number of drug cases given that Yavapai County was a major drug corridor, to the north I-40 and to the east I-17. Best like to work cases in Yavapai County, being a former football player at Bradshaw Mountain High School and his ailing parents still living there, he knew people and knew the intricacies of working with various agencies.

Best stood 6'2", lean, but muscled, with salt and pepper shoulder length hair (certainly not agency approved), looking more like a construction worker than a drug expert, comfortable in Prescott or Phoenix. He wore faded Levis a checkered red and white shirt and desert boots.

"Hey, Best, is that your agency issued Dodge Ram out there?" Fred joked with Joe. "And what brings you to God's country?"

"Ah, you know, I gotta come up here ever so often to keep you on your toes and check to see what kinda drugs flow through." Joe's smile covered most of the lower part of his face.

"Come on Joe, you're here for something specific, we all know that. Who did we pick up you want? Who's running stuff through here now?" Oriole smiled at knowing she was on target with his reason for being in town.

"Well, actually, we got word there's a bunch of meth flowing right now. An informant gave us info about an operation moving up to a couple pounds a week. I wanted to check in with you guys see what you'd heard and maybe run a joint operation to shut 'em down."

"Wow, couple pounds a week. That's a bunch. Usually it's by the gram. Where do you hear it's at? The last big operation shut down about eight big dealers. The biggest thing we got going right now is marijuana." Oriole and Fred were both excited by the opportunity for a change up in their case load.

"Our source says its north, up near Chino. Our confidential reliable informant (CRI) believes it's coming in by way of I-40 down 89. There's some kind of stopping point to break it up and then it's moving back up 89 to I-40 and down 89 to Prescott, Camp Verde and up I-17. We got some names and tentative locations I want to run by you to see if you heard of 'em. DEA contacted the Sheriff and he agrees to do a joint op. I asked for you two because I don't want to work with the Narcotics Task Force. I want someone out of the loop. I'm concerned it might be connected to an undercover. So, we'd have to be on the sly. You'd still have your regular case load and then work with me on this. I told the sheriff I wanted you two 'cause I can trust you. He said it was up to you to decide and if you said no, no harm, no foul. OK? In or Out?"

Fred looked at Oriole and raised his eyebrow in question to her. "Yeah, I'm in, Joe, can't speak for Fred even though I do most of the time." Oriole winked at Fred and rubbed her hands together with the possibilities of fun and games.

"Well, then don't speak for me. Crazy woman. I was busting druggies long before you were out of diapers and will be long after you're rocking on the porch of the retirement home. I don't want ya thinking you're going have all the fun. I'm in for a pound or two." Fred laughed at his own joke.

"Good, I knew you'd both be up for it. Want to grab some lunch. Then we'll see what we got to work with. I was thinking maybe the Prescott Brewing Company; I love their bread bowl. It's within walking distance."

"Walk? What're you saying? I got a horse, a motorcycle, a quad, a truck. Why would I walk anywhere?" Fred good naturedly chastised Joe.

"Alright, I been sitting for two hours. I need to move. You

drive, I'll meet you there. With parking, I'll probably be there first. What do you want to drink? Oriole, you riding or walking?"

"I'll walk down the hill with you. I got questions for you on the op. It's a good opportunity to get info since we can't talk at PBC."

Down the hill, Oriole and Joe caught up on times and people. He asked about Chalcey and couldn't believe she was already 13. She asked about his son and was surprised he was in college at California Davis. He inquired about Summer and Oriole asked after his ex-wife, Carole.

In general, the walk down hill was too short, but it gave each of them the opportunity to reconnect. Joe explained about the latest drug interdiction he was working on and the reason he had asked to have Oriole and Fred assigned to his task force. Methamphetamine was being smuggled across the border at an increasing rate and being transported through Arizona to points north, east and west. The DEA had informant information that Yavapai County was a major transfer site based on I-17 and I-40 traversing the county. Joe detailed the latest intel provided by a CRI where they believed the major transfers were taking place.

The special crimes unit of the Sheriff's office and the Department of Public Safety had made a huge dent in the drug trade on the corridor. The cartels had instituted new and better methods of hiding the dope and gaining a foothold in the trafficking once again. The DEA, through Joe's efforts, had determined that there might be a leak in one of the offices providing direct information to the cartel. Joe's task was to hand pick a few officers he trusted to join him in stopping the influx of meth and discover if and who in law enforcement was involved.

By the time Oriole and Joe reached PBC, he had finished his soliloquy and suggested they wait until after lunch to talk with Fred, just in case the walls had ears. They sat on the bench in front of PBC waiting for Fred, who had so far circled the block twice while they all but laughed out loud. Fred knew parking in the downtown area was a premium and still he insisted on driving. On his third trip, Oriole signaled she and Joe would wait inside for him.

After lunch, Joe and Oriole rode back with Fred and briefed him on the upcoming project. Naturally, Fred had more questions than there were answers.

10

SUMMER RETURNED TO BEAR RANCH after spending the day helping at Crimson Ranch. Joyce was home from the hospital and wouldn't be back on her feet for several weeks. Ron was ineffectual when it came to a mop and a broom. Chalcey entered the big country kitchen in a whirl, slamming down her back pack, throwing her coat on the closest chair, and yanking open the zero refrigerator.

"Whoa, girl, how was your day?" Summer could tell just by body language Chalcey was upset. Summer handed her a plate of homemade chocolate cookies and a glass of milk and sat down next to the chair buried in Chalcey's school residue.

"What's Hell, Summer?"

"Well, it depends on who you ask. Tell me the context of your question." Summer never talked down to Chalcey and in many ways Chalcey was more sophisticated than her peers because of it.

"Jenny asked me if I go to church. I said no we practice church every day. She told me if I don't go to church I'm going to Hell. So, does going to church save you from Hell? Or is this another one of those scare tactics used by so called Christians to increase their numbers?"

"Chalcey, what do you believe about God?"

"Well look at what God created, the beauty, the tiniest of creatures, the smells, the sights, and of course Red. God has to be good and full of love. God has to be patient. The world goes to war and kills the enemy, people rob from one another. Uhmm, I think God loves you, Marlowe, Oriole and me. So, in short, that's what I believe about God." Chalcey munched on cookies and drank long at her milk.

"Ok, so would the God you know send Oriole to Hell because she didn't go to Church? Summer challenged the premise Chalcey's schoolmate promoted.

"Mom saves people, she never raises her voice at me, she stopped that one time and rescued a raccoon baby, she donates time with Horses with Heart. So, no, God would see all the good she does and reward her. God wouldn't send her to Hell. Wait, I'm getting it." Chalcey's eyes opened wide and she started pacing around the kitchen. "Our God doesn't send good people to Hell and neither does Jenny's, even if she believes that. So, I'm not going to Hell if I do good things, clean my room, muck stalls, and obey you, Marlowe and Oriole. So, Jenny is full of manure."

"It isn't that she's full of manure. She is full of what others have told her rather than, like in your case, full of what you discern by using your noggin. If there comes a time when you want to go to church, you can. We've all had this discussion over each generation and we've all decided to let the newest generation decide on her own what she wants to do about religion. My parents let me choose and I chose Shamanism. I let Marlowe decide, she chose Buddhism. Marlowe let Oriole decide and she hasn't. So, Oriole will let you decide, if and when, you want. So, tell me what you think about thinking through issues?"

"Summer, I'm the luckiest kid in the whole world. I'm given the opportunity to think things through and apply what I've learned to situations. I know I'm not always going to be right, but I've got skills that Jenny may never have because her parents tell her what to believe and what to think. She doesn't use her noggin because she doesn't know how to question and seek answers. Yep, I'm one lucky kid."

Chalcey almost strutted across the kitchen and threw her arms around the seated Summer. "Well little miss lucky, how about getting out of your school clothes and getting your chores done. Maybe if you hurry you could help me over at Crimson because I have to go finish some things. Then we'll have time to get supper on."

Summer reflected on each of the generations' growth and enlightenment and felt her heart swell with pride in seeing it in Chalcey. She acknowledged 70 years of diversity paid off in the fourth generation and at that moment she wanted Marlowe and Oriole to share Chalcey's accomplishments still knowing they were busy with the day's work; it could wait.

11

ORIOLE, JOE AND FRED convened in the CID conference room to go over basics without going into detail due to the belief there might be a microphone and recorder in the room. At lunch they had agreed not to discuss the project at the office and to meet up at staggered intervals at the ranch, knowing it was probably the only really safe place in the county. Oriole and Marlowe regularly swept the house, bunk house, and office for listening devices after a bad experience of Marlowe's several years back where an overzealous soon-to-be ex-husband of a client had bugged the house and Marlowe's office.

Oriole had called Summer to say company was coming and a bag of groceries compliments of the guys would be arriving shortly, and to put aside the chili for another night. Summer and Chalcey finished chores and set the table for two extra, waiting for word on exactly what they were going to have for supper.

"Summer, it's always so good to see you. How have you been? Whipping that little girl in shape?" Joe affectionately greeted the family matriarch.

"Joe! Oriole just said company. She wouldn't say who. You're not company, you're family. Have been ever since that Mexican witch." Summer hugged Joe standing toe to toe and seeing eye to eye.

"Do you think we can turn your family room into a war room

later? We need privacy, and Oriole said it'd be OK. You know DEA will pay for the use and for the groceries." Joe could only assume Oriole had not seen the necessity of informing her grandmother of the purpose of his visit.

"The government isn't about to pay, any money will come from you directly. I know that. Stay as long as you need, eat as much as you want, forget the reimbursement, we'd have to fill out form this and form that and wait two years to be turned down." Summer chuckled at the reality of dealing with a bureaucracy and knowing the goodness of Joe's intentions.

"So, what's in this bag of goodies for supper?" Summer posed.

"Fred said get something unusual, that y'all don't usually have, so I picked up a trout, salad makings and fresh asparagus. He said he'd get the barbeque going and fix it." Joe started unloading the groceries and Summer and Oriole started putting together supper.

After the last scrap of trout was gone, dishes put in the dishwasher, the three officers adjourned to the family room, while Marlowe sat down with Chalcey to help her with her homework and Summer went out to the barn to check on the goat who was due any day.

"The CRI thinks one of the guys assigned to the task force is dirty." Joe began over a glass of wine. "He said the amount of dope is always short when he measures, but never when anyone else does. We think the guy has ties to the cartel and we're afraid he is either using or skimming." Joe poured a glass for each of the others and set up the laptop with a secure wireless connection.

"Do we know who this guy is?" Fred asked as they cleared off the six foot mahogany, hand carved table. "How reliable is this CRI? Does he have anything to lose?" Frequently, CRI's worked off charges by helping the cops and it was always a concern about whether or not the informant was making stuff up to clear themselves.

"Ever heard of JD Norman? He's on loan from Pima County? Apparently, he's some hot shot know it all? Loaned out because no one there would work with him?" Joe looked at Oriole and Fred for confirmation.

"Yeah, he's in the task force. Heard bad things about him, but never saw hard proof." Fred acknowledged the officer had a rep.

JD Norman was a 15 year veteran of law enforcement in four

different states and five different jurisdictions. He had been married so many times even he lost count. On his off time, he would be found in a local dive drinking most of the night. He thought of himself as a lady's man and more than likely that was why he couldn't keep track of the women he had married. Usually, he would move on before his bosses got around to firing him. Several times, the supervisors would give him the option of resigning rather than going through the hassle of firing him.

"Well, I'm keeping an open mind, but I'm not turning my back. The concerns we have are that there are several unsolved deaths relating to undocumented aliens that seem to fall on his doorstep. Plus, word has it he always knows where the strikes'll be and the take is always small potatoes compared to some of the other warrants he's not involved in. What we want to do is set up something and see if it falls into that category, and if so, then we kinda know going in we need more than just watching our backs. Our CRI will set up a pound or two and get word to him that it's ready to go down. We'll be on the street when it does and keep an eye out, if it comes up short, we think we can plan around JD. If not, oh well." Joe finished with the computer and explanation as Fred and Oriole finished their wine. "Let's finish up and I'll get back to town and find a room."

"Joe, you can't very well hang around the office. You might as well stay here and use this as your base. The bunkhouse is empty. You and Fred, if he wants, can stay there. It's certainly better than a hotel room and no hotel can match Summer's breakfasts." Oriole made the offer looking for a double-edged benefit. It would be easier to plan and organize if they were all together and it was nice to have Joe back in her space even if she was a little nervous about it.

"Fred, whatta ya say? Do you snore? Are you scared of the boogey man?" Joe kidded.

"Snore? You're the one who snores. Remember in Ruidoso last year? You took the roof off. I had to buy ear plugs." Fred poked at Joe with the half-truth.

"Oriole, do we need to talk first with Summer? I sure don't want to impose. If we were to do that, why can't we use the bunkhouse as the base? Then there'd be less disruption for the family."

"I cleared it with Summer. Use the house or the bunkhouse. Doesn't matter. Can we ask who your CRI is?"

"Ok. Sure. The CRI is Mark Littleton."

"What? The crew chief out at the pipeline? Fred exclaimed.

"Sounds like you already know him."

"He was forth coming about events on a murder we're working. You don't think they're connected, do you?" Fred felt the excitement mount.

"Tell me about your murder." Joe asked.

Fred and Oriole shared all they knew about the murder, while Joe gave them everything he had on Littleton. The cross referencing provided a great deal of information neither had previously. Now that the two cases were connected, the newly formed task force had a direction and a strategy for action. Joe planned on a meeting with Littleton, while Fred and Oriole projected a meeting with the widow Stutz and finding the new friend of the deceased, Gary.

12

"MARLENE, this new friend of your dad's, can you tell us how to get ahold of him?" Oriole called the daughter of the deceased.

"Gary, Gary, something. He's an architect locally. He's on a bunch of committees here. One is the Sharlot Hall Museum. You could get ahold of them for how to find him. But can you be discreet? I don't want Daddy's name dragged through the mud." Marlene was almost in tears.

"We just want to ask some questions. We'll be as discreet as possible. It might help if you could give us a little more information on Gary. That might help us be even more discreet. Did you look through your dad's stuff to see if there might be a name and phone number?" Patience was a virtue, but Oriole's was running out with the family.

"Well, I never looked for a phone number. If Daddy had it, it would either be in his cell phone or his PDA or maybe on his desk. Where's his phone and PDA? Do you have them, 'cause I don't have either."

"This is the first we heard his phone and PDA are missing. Can you give us the makes, models and carrier, please." Patience was replaced by teeth grinding.

"Well, I'm sorry. There have been so many details. I just forgot about the phone and PDA. I'll get the make and model and the number. The carrier is the same as everyone's here. It'll only take me a minute. Oh, here, here are some phone numbers in Daddy's hand writing. This one is for Gary. I don't know anyone else named Gary so this must be it."

"Thanks, Marlene, I know this has not been easy for you. I appreciate all your help. Things will sometimes fall through the cracks. We'll get through this together. You wouldn't happen to have the most current bill would you, does your bill show recent calls? That might save us getting a subpoena." Oriole had taken a moment to put herself in Marlene's shoes and relaxed back to her compassionate self.

"The bill does show calls made and received. We'll have to separate Daddy's from the others because they all come in on the same bill."

"That's okay, can you fax me a copy of the bill then it'll be easier to eliminate the company personnel." Oriole was ready to get on with locating Gary.

"Sure, I'll just fax you a complete copy. Names are next to the number as to who is assigned which number."

Fred had taken the time to review the will and insurance policies of Marvin Stutz before placing a phone call to the widow. "Mrs. Stutz, this is Detective O'Neill. I need to ask a few questions on follow up. Is now a good time?"

"Well, no time is a good time, but what do you need to know?" Fred could hear the reluctance in Mary's voice.

"It looks to me that the insurance policies go to your children, and everything else to you. Is that right?"

"Yes, there's a $250,000.00 insurance policy to Jeremy and Marlene and the house here, the cars, the condo Marvin bought for himself and the one for Marlene, some stocks, the paintings, jewelry, heirlooms, and everything else is mine. And it should be, after putting up with his lifestyle all these years." Her voice was just a bit snippy.

"Ma'am can you tell me how much the estate is worth?" Fred refused to allow her to divert him.

"There is no estate. My name was on everything, joint tenants with right of survivorship. Nothing will be probated because I survived Marvin and it's mine now." He could almost see her stomp her Jimmy Choos.

"Yes, ma'am that's why I'm calling. It looks to me like the holdings would run close to two million dollars excluding the insurance policy. Am I close?" Fred wanted her to know he had done his homework.

"Well, that seems high. I certainly haven't had time to add it all up. I've been a little busy with arrangements. What difference does it make anyway?"

"I'm just doing some follow up, Mrs. Stutz."

"I wish you would quit calling me that. I haven't used his name for years. Call me Mary or call me Ms Stillwell. Okay?" Mary's voice had taken on an edge even the phone lines couldn't disguise.

"The difference is we're trying to find out what happened to your late husband, who might benefit from his death, and who might have had a motive to kill him." Fred decided not to pull any punches in laying it on the line for her.

"Wait just a minute here. You're not saying I had a motive, are you?" Indignation poured forth from her. "Why that's the most ludicrous thing I've ever heard. You're out of your mind. Don't you have anything better to do with your time than hound me. I've just lost my husband and you're accusing me of killing him. I demand you leave me alone or I'll be forced to contact your supervisor." With that, she slammed down the phone.

Fred sat at his desk, holding a dead phone, looking smug as Oriole walked by. "Just what canary did you swallow." Oriole smiled at her partner.

"It gets curiouser and curiouser. Shakespeare was right, me thinks the lady doth protest too much. Let's bump the grieving widow up the list of possibles." Fred grinned at Oriole.

"Tell me why?"

"Two million whys, that's why. She gets it all except for the kids get an insurance policy. Nothing goes through probate because of the way it was titled and deeded. Everything was in both names, even though she despised him." Fred was stacking the paperwork in an expando file.

"I have what I think is THE Gary's phone number, plus Marlene faxed over cell phone records. Did you know his phone was missing and that PDA thing-a-ma-bob? Why do people have the PDA anyway? Can't they keep up with life with a plain ole fashioned calendar? My life is too complicated as it is, what would I do with two more things to keep up with." Oriole was bemoaning progress.

"Let's call and see if it is "THE" Gary. Then let's compare cell phone records with the numbers we know and see who was the last to call Marvin. Which do you want live phone or quiet, boring paper?" Fred was trying to work his subtle magic on Oriole.

"Oh, no you don't, boring paper is my cup of tea. You call. I know you, you're trying to make me do what you don't want to by making it sound horrible. Then I follow your suggestion and end up regretting it. No, siree, no, siree. This girl ain't falling in that trap again."

"Ok. OK. I'll do the phone stuff. No problemo."

"Wait a minute; are you trying to snow me. Did you really want to do the phone and really wanted me to do the paper? No, I'll take the phone you take the paper."

"Sure, whatever you say." Fred could hardly keep from laughing out loud at messing with her mind.

"Too easy. If you fold like that, that means you really didn't want me to do paper because the phone'll be easier. No. Nope. Nada. I'll do paper and you do phone." Oriole's years with Fred convinced her he was working her, but she just wasn't sure which way.

"We'll flip a coin." Fred suggested.

"Oh, sure that double headed nickel in your left pants pocket. Not even. If we flip, it'll be with my coin, not yours, you sneaky devil." Now Oriole thought she had figured out what he wanted all the time and was ahead of him and the game.

"You guys could have had it done by now. Quit arguing and just do it." Lieutenant Miranda chastised them as he walked through CID.

Oriole whispered across her desk to Fred, "you did that on purpose, you knew he was coming. I'm remembering this for future reference, you dog."

Fred was overcome with laughter and picked up the phone to call "the" Gary. "Gary, this is Detective O'Neill with the sheriff's office. Do you have a moment, I'd like to ask you some questions?"

"Sheriff's Office? What can I do for you?" The voice was a deep bass with a definite southern drawl.

"We're doing some background checks. Do you know a Marvin

Stutz?"

"Oh." A long pause created more questions for Fred.

"Well, do you know him?"

"Well as a matter of fact, we were acquainted. What's this about?"

"Would it be convenient for you to come down to the office to discuss this further?" Fred was signaling Oriole with a thumb's up.

"Come down? What can't we discuss over the phone? I'm really busy here." There was a certain put-offishness about the inquiry.

"Perhaps we could come there. It won't take long. Tell me where you are, we can be there in 10 minutes." Fred wasn't about to let this guy get away.

"Uh, no. I'm busy right now. Tell me what your schedule is this afternoon. I could probably get away this afternoon." There was a hint of panic in his voice.

"How about 2:00? Would that work for you?" Fred wanted to pin him down as soon as he could.

"Fine. I'll be at your office. Is that the one on Gurley?"

"Yes. If you'll just go to the door next to the constable's office and ask for Detective O'Neill. They'll call me. I'll see you at 2:00. Thanks." Fred hung up and clapped his hands.

"Are we excited about something?" Oriole looked up from her review of the cell phone records.

"He's too busy for us at his office. Bullshit. He'll be here at 2. See anything in the phone records?"

"Marvin got a total of 15 calls the day he went missing. Four from Marlene, which matches what she said. Three from Littleton. Two from Smith. The rest are a variety. What's Gary's cell and office number?" Oriole tapped her pencil against her teeth.

"We only have office on "the". Remind me to get his cell phone number when he gets here. Do any of them come from California or Tucson?" Fred was thinking in terms of family.

"Two from a California area code. That's probably Mrs. Stutz. None from Tucson or to." Oriole responded.

California would be either 'Mary, or Ms Stillwell' as I was informed. What about out going?"

"Six out going. One to Littleton, two to Smith. Two local. One to California." Oriole looked up from her copies of Stutz's records.

"We need to follow up on those local. Betya dollars to donuts, at least one is to "the"." Fred could hardly contain his glee in the new found records.

"We've got time to meet with Joe, if you want before our meeting with 'the.' How about lunch, I'm starving. All this reading is making me hungry. Let's call Joe and grab some Chinese." Oriole was indeed hungry, but also wanted to bring Joe up to speed on what they'd found.

At lunch Joe briefly explained the plans so far. He had set up a sting buy with meth using the CRI and planned it during the shift work of JD Norman. He had acquired a good deal of meth for the buy and had previously measured the amount, recorded it and used a special dye to mark the package and the meth. His plan was to set up the buy with his CRI and to use Fred or Oriole to complete the process.

Unfortunately, Joe was unable to get Fred or Oriole and because of his concern about an insider, he contacted a DEA friend to join him, JD, and the rest of the Narcotics Team.

The six met at the Village parking lot close to 7 pm. The CRI was patted down, pockets turned, socks checked and coat squeezed. His car was checked by the drug Canine dog. The money was marked and copied. Everything was set for a buy to go down at 9:30 p.m. out near Embry Riddle University. Joe and JD rode together. The other four split up and took two cars. The CRI went by himself. They had outfitted him with the latest video camera disguised as a key fob.

The team was in place, behind the new grocery store out on Willow Creek, waiting for the buy to go down. The CRI had enough cash to buy an ounce of meth. That much meth on the streets would meet the needs of hundreds of users especially after it was cut with baking powder or cornstarch.

Littleton, the CRI, waited in his truck in a semi-crowded part of the parking lot. The seller was to pull his car in next to Littleton's and make the transfer. At 9:45, a late model BMW pulled in next to Littleton. Littleton figured nobody in a Beemer would be selling and paid little attention to the car until there was a rap on the window.

"I'm lost. Can you give me directions to the Grand Canyon?" The code that the seller had given to Littleton on the phone earlier in the day.

"Sure, I'll draw you a map." Littleton replied and slipped the money in an envelope he handed to the guy in the Beemer.

"The directions look easy. Here you can have your envelope back." And the dope was put inside the envelope and passed back to Littleton.

For the next day, Joe had scheduled a late afternoon meeting with Littleton away from the pipeline and away from the office to maintain some secrecy. The rock pit was secluded, yet frequently used by locals for target practice. "Your work has been real important to us. I appreciate the position you're in. Tell me what's been going on since Mr. Stutz was killed."

"Smith has been real busy, but not at work. I've been keeping an eye on his comings and goings. I think something big is happening soon. He seems to be antsy. I'm keeping my distance 'cause I don't trust him. He'd soon stick a knife in ya as look at ya. I'm telling you he's dangerous. I saw him kill a dog that wandered in the yard, just because the dog wouldn't leave. He beat it to death and didn't even bat an eye. This guy is off the charts." Littleton paced back and forth in front of Joe's SUV.

"Anything else going on that you've seen?" Joe asked.

"Seems every time I see him he has a different car. What's that all about? Also, he has several cell phones, the company one and then another that is real small he keeps in his pocket. I've seen him use it instead of the company one several times toward the end of the day. A couple weeks back, I was downtown for an art festival and it was real crowded. He was on the plaza sitting on a bench like he was waiting for someone. It's that bench over by the gazebo. That's where all the bikes park when they're in town. Some biker dude walked over and sat down and had a cigarette, then got up and left, put something in his saddlebags and roared on down Montezuma."

Joe considered the possibilities, but without more didn't see how the incident on the plaza was significant. Littleton left. Joe took a few practice shots, took time to clean his gun and placed some phone calls before he left to give Littleton time to get back to work.

13

THE RECEPTIONIST CALLED FRED to tell him someone was there to see him, but refused to give his name. Fred walked down the hall and looked through the glass door to see a tall, gray haired man of about 50 waiting in the lobby pacing back and forth in front of the bench. Fred walked out to greet him, "Gary? I'm Detective O'Neill, thanks for coming down, let's go back to my office. Detective Wolfe is waiting for us." Fred made a correct assumption the distinguished gentleman was indeed "the".

"Detective Wolfe, this is…. I'm sorry, Gary, what's your last name?"

"Do you really need this information? I'm here trying to save everyone embarrassment and confusion. I came here voluntarily. What do you want to know about Marvin?" The anger and sarcasm were apparent in his voice and actions.

"Let's have a seat. Can I get you something to drink?" Fred made nice in an attempt to diffuse the situation.

"What and give you my DNA or fingerprints? Look what do you want of me. I barely know Marvin. I met him a few months ago. We had a couple drinks and that's all. Is there anything else you want? I'm busy." His right hand went to his hip and his left flailed in obvious frustration.

"Let's have a seat. Can I get some information from you?

Chapter 13

What's your last name?" Fred sat down opposite Oriole leaving the third chair next to her empty for "the".

Gary sat down, crossed his legs, checked the crease on his gabardine slacks. "My name is Patterson, Gary Patterson."

"Mr. Patterson, we appreciate your assistance. I understand this is sensitive. We'll honor that. When did you meet Mr. Stutz?" Oriole had her pen out and was making notes of nothing important, in order to keep Mr. Patterson from clamming up.

Patterson seemed to be putting on a "gay" persona. First, he was using gestures that lots of gays use and next he was exhibiting heterosexual motions. Either he was conflicted or he was playing a part.

"I met Marvin a few months back on Whiskey Row. Maybe January, February. Something like that. I bought him a drink, he bought me one. We exchanged phone numbers. We met a few times after that. We seemed to have lots in common. He was busy and I was busy. That's all I know." Apparently, the gabardine slacks needed re-checked, because he grabbed the crease at the knee and re-aligned it.

"Did Mr. Stutz seem concerned about anything?" Oriole asked looking sideways at "the".

"Concerned? What do you mean? What are you looking for here?"

"Did Mr. Stutz confide in you about any troubles he was having?" Fred tried to move the questioning along.

"Wait. What is this about? Where is Marvin? Why are you asking me these questions?" 'The' had uncrossed his legs, leaned forward placing both forearms on the table and glared at Fred.

"Mr. Patterson, I'm sorry to inform you, Mr. Stutz is deceased." Oriole gently explained.

Patterson whipped back in his chair, placed a hand on his forehead, then on his mouth, then drew in a deep breath, and turned deathly white. His demeanor seemed to indicate he wasn't aware of Marvin's death, but after years of watching suspects, Fred was dubious. "Deceased? When? How? Oh, my God. How did you come across me?"

"His daughter thought you might be able to shed some light on it." Fred non-committingly said raising the ever present one eyebrow in question.

73

"Marlene? What does she have to do with this?"

"How well did you know Marvin Stutz?" Oriole brought the questioning back on topic.

"I didn't really know him. I mean, we were just new friends. Do you understand? We liked similar things, doing things together, hanging out. He was a great cook. We enjoyed each other's company. We were not an item or anything like that. You have to understand Prescott is a small town, any gossip of this could ruin me. I don't know what you want from me. What else are you looking for?" Patterson had begun to stammer and sweat, even though the air was on in the interview room.

"Mr. Patterson, when was the last time you spoke to Mr. Stutz? And could we get your cell phone number to cross check records?" Fred was working to get "the" back on track.

"Spoke to Marvin? Umm, must have been last Tuesday. I think I called him and he called me back. I'll give you my card it has my cell phone and office phone." He pulled out a business card from a slim, elegant wallet. "We were planning on getting together for a drink about 9. But we never firmed up where. I didn't see him." The's obvious nervousness was palpable, not unusual for a novice at investigations. He shifted in his seat and couldn't seem to get comfortable and those damn stylish gaberdine slacks kept shifting.

"Did he seem worried about anything? And if he was, would he have shared that with you?" Oriole wanted to keep the interview moving.

"Worried? How would I know that? It wasn't like we were bosom buddies. Oh, God, did I really say that? What I meant was Marv and I didn't share intimate thoughts. Well, what I mean is, what I'm trying to say is. Can't you help me here? I'm having difficulty putting into words what we were to each other."

Both Oriole and Fred waited without interrupting Patterson knowing that the longer they waited the more information they might obtain.

"We had planned a long weekend trip to Las Vegas, no date certain. We thought it would be an opportunity to get to know each other away from the nosy interference of Prescott. We were both mature and had a sense that this could be a long-term friendship. We didn't want to rush it. I had some big jobs coming up that I needed to finish before we could take the time to get away. He had the pipeline to work on and felt he couldn't turn it over just yet. There were some problems out there that needed to be handled. So, we had to wait. Looks like we waited too long." Patterson finished sadly, brushing his hand across his face.

"Did he talk about his family?" Fred wanted to keep the interview moving.

"You mean that money grubbing wife and those two ungrateful kids?"

"What did he say about them"?

"We talked a little about his situation, being separated and that she wasn't about to give him a divorce. He spoke a little about Jeremy and Marlene. I'd met Marlene once by accident I ran into them when they were at dinner and I was at the restaurant for a business meeting. Never met Jeremy. Wait. How did Marv die?" The shock was wearing off and Gary began processing information.

"We can't go into that right now. But it wasn't an accident." Fred didn't want to give more than he had to right at that moment.

"I'm having trouble thinking this through right now. My kids had met Marv and really liked him. My kids and his kids are okay with our life decisions. Mary was the only one who couldn't get past it and get on with her life and let him get on with his. What a loss. Do you have an information about services?" It was obvious that either Gary cared about the deceased, more than the wife, or he was a very good actor.

"The remains have not been released at this time." Oriole provided.

"Tell me about the problems out at the pipeline." Fred wanted to keep on keeping on.

"Troubles? Oh. Marv was pretty close about work. But several times when we would meet, he'd get phone calls that bothered him. I got the feeling that there was something happening that he didn't like, but he couldn't quite get a handle on it. It wasn't anything he said as much as what he did when he got these phone calls. And then there was this one time when he thought someone was following us when we were on our way to Sedona. You know? I think he was right. But I tried to cajole him when it happened. It was so Sherlock Holmes. Then he said something about getting an auditor in because he was concerned about missing inventory, but he wasn't sure whether to go to the company or just hire someone out of his pocket. I think, now he never said, but I think it might have had something to do with Marlene. He asked me for the name of a good accountant that could keep his or her mouth shut. That's what made me think it might have to do with Marlene. She was the office manage/ accountant out there. It seems like he would have asked her. But he said he didn't want to. "Gary finished and looked at both detectives for directions.

"Mr. Patterson, were there other instances of Mr. Stutz feeling threatened or afraid or anything like that?" Oriole asked as follow up to the incident in Sedona.

"Well, now that you mention it, it seems that there was an incident out at High Desert. We went out there together one Saturday to look at the plants for some work I had to do to make this project look natural with landscaping and such. I picked him up about nine and we stopped for a Starbuck's. There was someone in there he was worried about seeing, so I went in and got us coffees. He kept looking in the mirror to see if we were followed. There was a lot of traffic going out toward High Desert, so it was hard to tell if there was someone back there. But he was real edgy. I gave him a bad time about it cause I thought it was because of our life decision. Later I knew it wasn't about that, it was something else."

"What did you think it was about?" The conversation seemed to be moving toward something, but Fred wasn't sure what.

"That incident in Sedona and the one at High Desert, it seemed like someone was keeping an eye on Marv on his off time. But I don't know why and I don't really think he did either. I think if he had known, he would have told me. Not that we shared everything. But we did talk about stuff, ya know."

"Anything else you can think of, Mr. Patterson?" Oriole was concerned they'd got all they were going to get.

"No. I'll think about some of the places we went, things we did. If anything comes up, I'll be sure to let you know. I appreciate your kindness. You treated me with dignity, without judgment. Thank you."

After they had escorted Gary out, Fred and Oriole reconnoitered back in the office. "Do you think he is playing a part for our benefit?" Oriole posed.

"Like you mean he isn't really gay—is that what you're thinking?"

Chapter 13

"Fred, we've both come across lots of people of alternative life styles. Some are flamers, some are not. But flamers stay flaming. He couldn't figure out if he was or wasn't."

14

SUMMER AND CHALCEY fixed pork chops with scalloped potatoes, a crisp salad with homemade dressing, and fresh bread for supper for the 'troops' as Chalcey like to call the new additions to the Ranch. Chalcey was reveling in the attention from Fred and Joe, and making note of subtle changes in the people around her. "Summer, did you notice Oriole put on actual make-up today? She never does that. Do you think it's because of Joe?"

Summer half-snorted at the inquiry and turned her back to cough to cover before answering, "why do you think it's because of Joe?"

"Well, I've watched how Joe looks at her and how she looks at him. It's like you look at Doc Chris when he comes out to take care of the horses. "

"What? How I look at the vet? I don't look at anyone like you're talking about."

"Summer, you know you do. At the Equifest, you talked to him for hours. He was drooling all over you. I don't know why he didn't ask you out or you didn't ask him out. That's what I'm talking about."

"I think it's time to set the table, Chalcey. Let's get busy."

Joe, Oriole, and Fred got together for supper at the Ranch. Over dinner, they exchanged a light banter saving the meat of the investigation for later in the bunk house. By now they had turned the bunk house into a war room with poster boards and bulletins. Each of the officers took turns bringing the task force up to date on the latest discoveries.

"So, what's going on this weekend?" Joe asked after discussing the case.

"Well, Marlowe and I are taking in a movie and dinner." Fred sheepishly replied.

"Hey, that sounds fun. Can Oriole and I join you?"

"Whoa. Joe, I think he means they are going on a DATE. It'd be like having chaperons. Ummm. That might be fun. I can remember being a teenager and having too many noses in my business. Maybe I can turn the tables on Marlowe." Oriole was chuckling at the prospect.

"A date? Fred and Marlowe are going on a date?"

"No, it's not a date. We just going to the movies and dinner. It's not a date." Fred was stumbling all over himself to convince Joe and Oriole, as well as himself, it was not a date.

"So where are you taking her for dinner? Maybe Oriole and I will go watch."

"Quit with the razing or the date is off."

"I knew it. I knew it. It is a date." Joe continued to prod Fred.

"Ok. Joe, enough already. I don't want to see Marlowe lose out on the chance for a free meal 'cause we had fun at Fred's expense. Let's let the old folks have their social time before the rocking chair requirement sets in." Oriole wanted to tease Fred, but knew when to stop. "Anyway, maybe you, me, Summer and Chalcey can do something that will be even more fun."

"Ok. I'll let Fred off the hook. But I want a report tomorrow about the movie." Turning to Oriole, Joe said, "Just what do you have in mind for the four of us?"

"Chalcey wanted to do Out of Africa. Have you been out there recently? They have really made improvements, new animals and environments. Last time we were there the giraffes took carrots out of Chalcey's mouth. I had the video camera and it was great. We were talking about Mexican, but there's the Haunted Hamburger up in Jerome. Then we could look at the museum maybe." Oriole was updating Joe on possible plans as rapidly as she could without sounding anxious or overly interested.

"Let's leave Fred to stew in his own juice and go talk to Summer and Chalcey to see what they want to do. I promise I'll leave the DATE stuff alone." Joe's mouth curved in the tiniest of smiles.

As Joe and Oriole walked into the kitchen, they saw they had interrupted a discussion with Chalcey and Marlowe about the upcoming festivities Saturday night.

"No, Chalcey this isn't a date date. It's more like a get together." Marlowe was adamant.

"Well, what's the difference?"

"A date date is where people who are interested in a relationship are going out. A get together is where people who aren't in a relationship get together for fun." Marlowe continued to wipe the counters and put away dishes, while trying to make light of the questioning.

"Chalcey. How about you, Oriole, Summer and me doing a 'get together'?"

Joe interposed giving Marlowe a much needed break.

"Like what?"

"Oriole said you liked Out of Africa. Maybe go there and then to a museum and dinner." Joe reiterated what Oriole had suggested.

"Can we get dressed up, Oriole, can I wear some make up like you have on?"

"I don't have make up on. And, yes we can get dressed up. But no makeup." Oriole was smiling to herself about her 20 something 13 year old.

"Summer are you up for a 'get together' tomorrow?" Joe inquired of the Bear Ranch matriarch.

"A chance to get dressed up, go look at animals and go out for dinner? Sweet Mary, Joseph and little baby Jesus, I guess so!"

15

SATURDAY BROUGHT A LIGHT RAIN to the ranch, settling the dust and freshening the air. The horses were frisky, running back and forth in the pasture, calling to each other to play. The goat and her kid were romping in their pen. Chalcey felt the excitement of the critters as she mucked out the stalls with the help of Joe and Fred and fed Timothy hay to the horses and alfalfa to the goats. "Fred why do we give Timothy to the horses instead of alfalfa, like we do the goats?" Chalcey always had another question.

"Alfalfa gives the horses extra energy. Too much and they'll get real froggy. That goat needs it to produce milk for her kid. The Timothy is lower fuel and healthier right now for the horses. Come winter, you'll be feeding alfalfa to the horses to keep them warm." Fred seemed to always have an answer for Chalcey.

"Will we grow enough or do we have to lay up a store for winter?" Based on the syntax of her question, Fred could tell Chalcey'd been listening to Summer.

"It all depends, my little lumpkin. It all depends." Fred and Joe finished and they all trooped up to the expansive porch where ice tea, lemonade and cookies were waiting. Marlowe had gone into town to meet a client and Oriole rode in with her to get groceries. On the way, the 2nd and 3rd generation talked about the coming events and implications of dating friends.

"It's been so long since I've been on a date, I'm not even sure what to do any more. Is it like riding a horse or a bicycle? Do I just go with the flow? Should I just be me and if it goes well, OK and if not Fred and I can still be friends? What if he has some horrible twitch that I just can't overlook? Oriole, stop laughing and help me out here." Marlowe was truly perplexed and obviously distressed at the prospect of a real date.

"I'm not laughing at you, I'm laughing with you." Oriole was still chuckling under her breath.

"I'm not laughing, you imp."

"Look Marlowe, how long have you known Fred, twenty, thirty years? Granted you only know him in the context of horses, the ranch, and my work, but in all the times you've seen him and interacted with him, has he ever done anything that made you go, 'ugh, I don't like that'? Has he ever picked his nose and eaten it? Has he ever farted at the dinner table? You can't know everything about someone until you spend quality time with them. It builds each time you see them in different environments. You have to do things together to see if you want to do more. It's a process. I suggest you go slow and take your time."

"Oh, my God, I'm getting tutored by my daughter on dating. How weird is that? Don't you tell a soul or I'll take away TV for a month." Marlowe laughed with her gorgeous daughter at the irony on the situation.

"So, what are you going to wear? Hair up or down? Boots or sandals? A light cologne or a fruity one? Cleavage or conservative? These are all things to think about. You only get one first date, unless you're Reese Witherspoon." Oriole was enjoying her role as matchmaker.

"I don't know. I hadn't given it a thought. I figured I'd just get dressed and go. What? I have to plan ahead. I have to think through all this stuff. Why can't I just brush my hair and go? There's a lot to this dating stuff. Maybe I'll just stay home instead. It'd be so much easier."

"You are not staying home, and that's that. You will get ready and go and have a great time. Now what are you more comfortable in pants or dress?"

"Well, it's May, evening's will get chilly so, I guess pants."

"So, we'll look for dressy causal. Now, if you wear those fancy rodeo pants and the Lucheses, probably the black ones. Do they need polishing? How about the suede vest with that French cuff white shirt and those crystals that Eva made for you? OK. You're dressed. Hair. Up is so sophisticated, but down is soft and feminine. How about down this time? I'll even help you put in hot rollers and add a little curl. Now what's left? Perfume. You don't want to be overwhelming, but you want something fresh and light. Pheremone. Do you have any left? If not, you can use some of mine. Wow. I missed my calling. I should have been a date planner—you know like the wedding planner." Oriole was plainly pleased with her accomplishments.

"Oriole, don't you be so smug. Just you wait. It'll be my turn soon enough. I see how Joe looks at you. Then you think back to this conversation and remember payback's a bitch." Marlowe couldn't help but laugh out loud at the reversal in roles.

"Joe, got a minute?" Fred approached the make shift desk in the bunk house.

"Sure. What's on your mind?"

"Well. You know Marlowe and I are going to the movies and dinner. Can I ask you about this dating thing? I haven't dated in 30 or more years. Do we do dinner first or the movie first? Do I wear a suit or jeans? Do I buy her flowers? What the hell do I do?" Fred was pacing back and forth in front of Joe's desk, hands stuck in his pants pockets, clearly suffering through this ordeal.

"Oh, man, I hear you. Do you open the door or let her get in by herself? Do you pull her chair back or let her do it? Too many questions about this dating stuff. How are you most comfortable? Jeans and blazer? Boots and hat?

"I always wear blazer and jeans. I'm never without my hat. I only own boots."

"Then go with comfort and stylish. Are your boots clean—don't want horse shit on 'em. Forget the flowers, unless you wanted to get some for Summer and the girls. Dinner or movie first? Umm... Do the movie first, then dinner so you can relax and talk about the movie. Or ask her what she wants to do. Or provide both options and negotiate. You'll do fine. Go to have fun and relax and enjoy yourself. Don't make it too hard." Joe kicked back in his chair as he finished.

The evening found Chalcey, Oriole, and Summer in Marlowe's

bedroom suite helping her get organized for her "date" for the next day. "I've already decided what to wear, how to smell, what else do I have to do for this date?

"Marlowe, you should put a quarter in your boot." Chalcey offered from the four poster pine bed.

"What's a quarter in my boot do?"

"Well if you have to call home you can use your quarter."

"I've got my cell phone for that."

Oriole flipped a condom to her mother without a word.

"Oriole Wolfe! Shame on you." Summer chided.

"What was it? I missed it." Chalcey begged to be included in the joke.

"Chalcey, your mama is being a pickle. Never you mind." Marlowe hugged her granddaughter and kissed her on the head. "Oriole, you keep this you'll probably need it before me." Marlowe threw it back at her daughter.

"Come on Chalcey, what are you going to wear on our get together with Joe." Summer took Chalcey's hand and walked her to her room for a diversion.

"I'm going to wear that new outfit, the long skirt and vest, my boots and I think I'll wear my hair in a ponytail." Chalcey took her great grandmother to the closet to show her the selection.

"Good, Sweetie, let's make sure everything is ready. Knowing Joe, he'll be ready on time. Women in this family never keep a man waiting on purpose. Too often something else will come up that happens to forestall our presence. Shake a leg, girl get your stuff put together." Summer left to go finish up the evening chores.

Next morning Oriole and Summer were downstairs waiting when Joe walked in. "May I help you sir?" Summer good naturedly teased Joe who was dressed in pressed Levi's, shined boots and a suede blazer.

"Very funny, Summer. I'm here to take three of the best looking women out on the town."

"Chalcey. Joe's here for our date." Oriole called up to her daughter. The gangly thirteen year old had disappeared to be replaced by a charming, well dressed, sophisticated looking young lady. "Maybe I should go change so you all won't be ashamed of me." Oriole said as she smiled at her daughter.

Joe looked at Oriole, "you look fine to me. I like what you did with your hair." He turned to Summer and Chalcey, "you all look just great. I'm about the luckiest guy in town. Let's get going." He was hoping to get the parade over before Fred or Marlowe could remark about the festivities.

On Sunday afternoon, Joe's cell phone rang. "This is Joe."

"Joe. This is Lt. Montoya. Sorry to disturb your Sunday. Something's come up. You need to put the task force on notice. You'll be working for a while in Yavapai. Check your email for details. I was just concerned about the walls." Lt. Montoya hung up and Joe immediately checked his secure email and then got ahold of Oriole and Fred.

"Looks like we have another homicide. It very well could be connected to your DB. Name is Janelle Jankowski. Office Manager/Receptionist out at the pipe line. Found her dead this morning in her trailer. Looks like a drug overdose. Next of kin is some sister in Las Vegas. LVPD made notification. Sister is coming in tomorrow. SO has secured the scene and is holding everything for us and the ME. She had a trailer out in Chino. Let's take two cars in case we have to later split up tasks. My lieutenant called me because there is belief that this body might have something to do with out task force. Sorry to ruin your Sunday." Joe was sincerely apologetic while knowing Fred and Oriole put work first.

"Let me tell Summer and Marlowe to make sure they have Chalcey covered."

"I'll change and be out front." Fred was already moving toward the bunkhouse.

They arrived at the mobile home that sat in the county's jurisdiction. Fire and paramedics had already been and gone. The ME arrived in their dust.

Joe took the lead and assessed the trailer. It was a salmon color, faded with wind and sun exposure to a pale pinkish orange. A circular driveway paved with AB rock greeted visitors. A metal set of steps accessed the front door. Trash littered the thumbnail front yard—car parts, black garbage bags, paint cans, fast food sacks and remnants of a left over hot tub. The front door opened into the living room which was covered in more of the same litter minus the car parts. The carpet had long since lost its claim to beige, soiled with what looked like dog feces, oil, mud and tracked in cow manure. A blank spot the size of a couch sat in front of the picture window to the left. A 60" plasma TV adorned the wall straight ahead seemingly incongruous with the residence.

Off to the left, Joe could see what once was an open kitchen floor plan, now cluttered with packing boxes, pizza boxes, chairs, tables and dirty dishes. Moving down the hall, the three detectives encountered three doorways; the first was to a bathroom, the second to a bedroom about 9x12, and the last to the master bedroom.

They stood in the doorway of the master bedroom, eyes moving right to left in a circular motion. On the queen sized bed, with her feet dangling over the edge of the bed, lay Ms Jankowski. Within two feet of her right hand lay a syringe, dried blood on the needle. Next to her was her purse, a baggy of white powdery substance, and a notebook containing pay and owe information. A tourniquet circled her left bicep.

The detectives had put on gloves and booties to preserve the scene. Fred picked up the notebook that contained names and amounts. Typically drug dealers kept track of who owed and how much. Sometimes the amount owing could run in the thousands. When you think about it, fronting money for using drugs is pretty stupid. The user keeps using and can't ever get caught up because he needs another fix. The system is far worse than the loan shark who loans money with a high rate of interest.

Photographs and videos had already been taken of the scene before the detectives or ME arrived. Rod Culpepper moved quickly and professionally in checking the body temperature for time of death, which he placed at six to twelve hours earlier making time of death between midnight and six a.m.

The deceased was dressed in black nylons, a red mini skirt, stretch tube top in red and black swirls, black spiked heels, a red and black Swarovski crystal necklace lay on the bed, matching earrings were in her pierced ears, a synthetic ruby ring on her right ring finger and a knock off Rolex on her right wrist.

"Looks too pat to be a drug overdose." Joe ventured. "Doc, what's it look like first blush?"

"I try not to judge in the field. But there is petechia, which could mean a lot of different things, but I'll be looking for strangulation marks in the autopsy. Her watch is on her right wrist, the syringe next to her right hand. Does that mean she was right handed wearing her watch on the right instead of left or does that mean she was left handed and someone didn't know and put the syringe in the wrong place? Won't know til probably later. Right now, this is a suspicious death as far as I'm concerned. I'd treat it as a homicide til we know better." Culpepper finished his examination, nodded to the technician to bag her hands and get the body bag.

A systematic search of the bedroom turned up little of consequence: no scales, no baggies, no pipes, no other syringes and no other evidence of drug use. The evidence technician bagged and tagged the items on the bed to send to the lab for fingerprint and chemical analysis.

"The landlord found her this morning when he came to collect the rent. The front door was open, her car in the driveway, no one else around. He thought it odd that the door was open and she didn't respond to his hellos so he walked in calling her name. He found her and immediately left the house to call it in. He said she'd been here about five months, always paid in cash, never gave him any trouble. He said he planned on cleaning the place up because she seemed to plan on staying. He never noticed any drug activity and since he lost two other places to meth labs, he's real sensitive about that." Fred finished reading his notes from interviewing the landlord and looked at the other two detectives.

"I didn't notice any other track marks, no outward signs of drug use. Rod will be able to tell us more on that tomorrow after the post." Oriole provided.

"Let's divide this up. Oriole, you get ahold of Marlene Stutz and get what information you can. Fred, you call Smith/Walsh for info and I'll call Littleton. Let's get together at 5:00 or before at the bunkhouse and see what we have. I want to keep this under wraps as much as we can since it appears to be a drug incident. I don't want the narcs in on it for now." Joe finished with the assignments and the detectives left the mobile home.

That evening after supper of Shepherd's Pie, coleslaw and strawberry-rhubarb pie, the detectives collated the information they had accumulated and started a new homicide book.

Rod Culpepper called Joe's cell phone to give him an update on the post mortem. "Looks like there was an overdose of pure methamphetamine. But there's more: stomach contents inexpensive Pinot Noir, tossed salad with chicken strips. Besides the meth in her blood stream, I found Ecstasy. Best guess is with the wine. No surprise surgical implants size E. And the frosting on the cake she was smothered maybe with a pillow. So, someone wanted this girl dead."

"Ecstasy? The date rape drug? Would she have been incapacitated by the drug?" Joe was furiously writing to keep up with the preliminary information.

"Maybe at least groggy enough for someone to do what they wanted. But then why smother her? That's what I can't get to. Any thoughts?" Rod was more than perplexed.

"Maybe he or she was afraid the meth wouldn't be enough to kill her. How much was in her system?"

"Enough literally to kill a horse. Let me know if you need anything else. The report will be done by tomorrow and on your desk. Talk to you later." Rod finished the call and cleaned up the autopsy room.

The next day, Joe, Oriole and Fred convened in the parking lot of Frontier Village to update each other on the autopsy and investigation so far. "It's definitely murder, if anything it's overkill." Joe relayed the ME's findings to the other detectives and listened to what Fred and Oriole had found so far.

"Smith says he was camping this weekend. Solo. Got back last night about 8:00. Hadn't seen Janelle since Friday at work. He said she had plans to go out Saturday night, but he didn't know where. He didn't have cell service where he was camping—up near Flagstaff. So, no alibi." Fred relayed his findings.

"Littleton said he saw her Friday, but she didn't mention anything about a date or going out at all, in fact he said she was grumping because she didn't have anything to do last weekend." Joe added his intel from the CRI.

"Well, I got lots more than you guys. Send a woman to do a man's job and it gets done right the first time." Oriole rubbed salt in the wounds. "Marlene said Janelle was particularly bummed on Thursday and Friday. Seems she had a date lined up and it was a bust. Then Marlene gets a call from her on Saturday asking if Janelle can borrow Marlene's red purse 'cause, here we go, Janelle has a hot date. Marlene tried to find out who and what the agenda was but Janelle blew her off gently enough to get the purse and not reveal anything. Marlene thought Janelle didn't want her to know because it was someone they both knew. And you know that's a small list. Janelle got to Marlene's about 6:30 Saturday night, dressed like we saw, but with a little black fur cape thing. Marlene thinks it was

Chapter 15

rabbit. We didn't find a rabbit stole at the house. So, find the rabbit, find the killer? Here's something else, Marlene had to do some work Saturday morning out at the pipeline and saw Smith working on some equipment. So, sounds like someone isn't totally truthful." Oriole finished her rendition of titter-totter Marlene's information.

"Sounds like we might need to double team Smith to get some more information. He's probably out at the pipe line. Why don't I take Oriole and see what I can get from him?" Fred seemed to want to supplement his incomplete interview with Smith.

"Why don't you take me? What is that? To see what you can get from him? What am I, milk toast? Why don't I take you out to the pipe line and show you how to thoroughly do an interview to fill in all the blanks." Oriole joked with Fred knowing if there was information that was contradictory it was because someone lied and there were two things that made Fred mad: a liar and a thief.

Fred and Oriole headed out to the pipe line planning their strategy along the way.

16

"MR. SMITH, could we have a word with you? We need to follow up on some information about Ms Jankowski." Fred spoke ingratiatingly hoping to instill trust and confidence and get what he came after.

"Can't you see I'm busy? Why don't you leave me alone?" Smith's obnoxious attitude surfaced.

"Just a question or two. Where did you camp up near Flagstaff?" Oriole moved forward with questioning.

"What? Where? Ahh... up near Mund's Park." Smith stuttered a reply.

"Do you have a receipt from a campground?" Oriole continued to press for answers while Fred took notes.

"No. I camped off the grid. What the hell's going on?" Smith's impatience came through.

"When did you leave for your trip?" Fred chimed in.

"I left Friday right after work. Do I have anyone to prove it? No. I was alone. I like being alone then I don't have to deal with idiots like yous." Impatience pushed to obnoxious.

"Did Janelle date anyone from the pipe line?"

"Are you thinking I had something to do with her death? Is that it? Let me tell you, she's not my type. Yeah big hooters, but nothing else. Why she was so ugly she'd make a freight train take a dirt road." Smith started laughing at his own joke, but laughed by himself.

"Mr. Smith. Did you see Janelle this weekend?" Oriole came right out and asked the question they had been skirting around.

"No. I didn't see her after Friday afternoon." Stubbornly, Smith almost yelled at the detectives.

"So, if someone says they saw you with her, are they mistaken?" Oriole plied one of the established interview techniques—box the suspect in the corner with what you think happened and see if they bite.

"Who? Who said that?" Smith's reply was not quite an admission, but pretty darn close. "Where was this supposed to be?"

"I'm the one asking questions here. Would they be mistaken?"

"I'm done talking to you. You want something else talk to my lawyer." Smith stormed off in the direction of the offices.

"Nellie. He was hot under the collar. Think we can find that person who saw them together?" Oriole took a deep breath to calm herself, while Fred snapped his notebook closed and both headed to the SUV.

"She was all dolled up. She had a date. She ate supper of salad and chicken strips and cheap wine. That wasn't at home. So, we start with Chino and move toward Prescott. We'll find him/her, them. If it was Smith, Chino's too small. There's only like four dinner places that serve wine. Chances are better in Prescott or Prescott Valley. Let's see if we can pull credit cards on Smith and go forward instead of backward on this. If there are receipts over the weekend, then we can go talk to the bartender or the waitresses." Oriole used her feminine observations and knowledge to brainstorm out loud a plan of action.

"I agree with you, she had a date and went out and came home. I'll look through her purse for matches or receipts. Maybe she paid or picked up matches. Maybe you could check for credit cards for her and Smith. Joe, I think Littleton might be able to provide more info given what we have so far. Maybe hit him again? What do you think?" Fred was also brainstorming out loud and falling into his pattern of being in charge without offending Joe.

"Whatever we can do back at the war room let's do, so we can keep a low profile. The evidence has to be here, so go for it. Let's see about dinner and a de briefing afterwards. I'll call Summer and see what we need. Oriole you go on out to the ranch and Fred that red purse will look good with your red, white and blue Western shirt and bolo." Joe handed out assignments in a low key and smiled at his joke.

"Hey, Summer, Joe here. What do you need for supper? Milk, bread, eggs, coffee, anything?" Joe had made an effort to help out with the shopping and the expenses since his arrival.

"Bless your heart, Joe Best. It's a mad house around here with Crimson Ranch needing help and trying to get ready for the rodeo and putting together a sweat for the cousin of Yellowhorse, why I could jump in the lake pull water up over my head. Why not pick up a couple pizzas, some beer, milk's OK, but bread for sandwiches if y'all need 'em, and we're out of Jamaica Blue. Chances are you won't find it in town, we'll have to order it. So, I guess that covers it. What time do you expect everybody? Oh, let's have some ice cream. I made a batch of your favorite cookies. Nothing like chocolate mint ice cream with fresh chocolate chip and Macadamia nut cookies." Summer was pleased that Joe was so thoughtful to pick up supplies.

"You made those just for me. How wondermous. Now don't let Fred and Chalcey eat 'em all before I get home with supper. It'll take me an hour and they should all be there by then." Joe's smile carried through his voice.

Summer, with the alleviation of dinner planning, went out to the barn to help with the chores. Chalcey had fed the horses and was mucking the stalls when Summer picked up feed from the hay barn for the rest of the critters. Feeding a pig, a mama goat, 3 dogs, now one cat, that crazy raccoon and five chickens took a while.

"Hey, Summer. Do we need to help feed over at Crimson tonight? When will Joyce be back on her feet?" The ranch philosophy of kindness and thoughtfulness had rubbed off on Chalcey over the years.

"Joyce will probably never be fully back, so we might have to help Ron here and there. He's got the ranch part covered. It's the stuff around the house. I swear that man doesn't know a pot from a skillet or a glass from a cup and he sure doesn't know what to do with a mop. Joyce did everything for him. He can't even figure out how to make coffee. I wrote out directions for him. Tomorrow when I go over to check on Joyce, I'll see if he had fresh coffee or instant. Let this be a lesson to you for your future—know a little about a lot and a lot about a little. Then you'll never be solely reliant on anyone." Summer's advice brought Chalcey up short.

Chalcey leaned on the poop rake and pondered. "I don't plan on getting married, so I won't need to rely on anyone. I'm going to live with all of you. I'm going to college to become a vet so I can take care of animals, then I'll know a lot about animal medicine. If I need the toilet fixed, I'll call a plumber. If I need the roof patched, I'll call a roofer. If I need a lawyer, I'll call Marlowe. If I need a cop—well I'll call Oriole or Fred or maybe Joe. Then I'll be self-reliant. Will you teach me how to make coffee tonight, then that will be one more thing I know how to do."

Summer smiled at her great granddaughter's logic. "Coffee tonight. Tomorrow we'll deal with the toilet ourselves. I'll show you a trick or two. If you have a crescent wrench, a sawsall, a drill, a hammer, a screwdriver, a level and a ladder, girl, you can do most anything need'n done. Let's throw in some lessons on boiling water too."

17

ORIOLE AND FRED had divided up tasks to track down information on Janelle's last night of life. Fred had phone records from Marlene and credit card receipts by way of an emergency subpoena. Oriole had decided to do some follow up on the Stutz case while waiting for the records, rather than make wasted phone calls if the information came through on any purchases or phone calls.

"We got him." Fred's exuberance burst forth. "He made three phone calls to Janelle's cell phone. One Friday night and two on Saturday. What about the credit card?" He turned to Oriole.

"Friday, gas at the Express Stop. And lookee here. Dinner at Zeke's Saturday night. $42.88, must be for two. Got that picture of Janelle and a driver's license picture of Smith?"

"Right here."

"Let's go to Zeke's. Want me to drive this time?" Oriole's long experience with Fred told her different, but she couldn't help herself. She had respected Fred's and Marlowe's privacy by not asking about the 'date date'. But curiosity was killing her. She knew better than to broach it with Fred if he didn't bring it up, so she'd have to wait and get it from Chalcey, Summer or God forbid, Marlowe. Fred did seem upbeat and happy. He had been humming a tune all day that kept repeating in her head.

"Could we talk to the manager?" Fred asked the waitress at

the register.

"That would be me until Jim comes on at 5:00. What can I do for you?"

"This is Detective O'Neill, I'm Detective Wolfe. We're with the sheriff's office. Were you on duty Saturday night about 8:30 p.m?"

"Jim and I both were. Saturdays are real busy."

"We're trying to find anyone who can tell us if a couple was in here. I have what we call a photo lineup of six males and another of six females. Could you look at them and tell me if you recognize anyone?" Fred pulled the line ups from a file folder and had the manager read the admonition and sign it.

"That lady there was here with a guy. Let's see they sat in section b, table 5 and had prime rib and chicken, beer and wine. She was wearing a real git up. Red and black. The guy she was with—a real looker, but kinda rough. Yeh, that's him #5. He ordered Corona and was kinda mean to her. I wanted to tell her to take a powder, that no guy that treats a woman like that is worth it, but I minded my own business."

"The credit card says 8:30 p.m. did they leave right then or stick around for music?"

"They left as soon as I gave them the credit card back. He paid. He was in some hurry. She hadn't even finished her wine and he was at the door. He'd spent most of the dinner on the phone. Rude. Some of the stuff we see."

"Thanks. Can we get your name and contact information in case we need more from you?" Oriole's excitement mounted.

Back in the SUV, Oriole put in a call to Joe. "Pay dirt. They were together at Zeke's. Let's wait to pick him up until we have just a little more. What about a search warrant for his car? We got hers. Let's go over it with a finetooth comb, see if anything shows up then maybe approach the county attorney for a search warrant for his car. Fred and I are on our way back to the SO. Maybe 10 minutes."

"I'll call the county attorney's office for the on-call deputy to see if we have enough for a search warrant. What else are you thinking about?"

"I don't know. We have eye witnesses. Phone records. Credit card records. How about DNA? What about going over her place again for his DNA or fingerprints. Weren't there a bunch that weren't hers? Maybe that could at least tie him to the house." Oriole was grasping for straws and knew it. There just had to be something solid to tie him to Janelle's murder." What about that second phone he had? Maybe I can call Marlene and get a lead on it."

"I'll call the technician and see about fingerprints. There were no skin fragments under her fingernails and no sign of recent sexual activity. There might be DNA like in the bathroom or on the syringe. I'll ask the tech when I talk to him. See you when you get here."

18

SMITH WAS PACING back and forth in front of his truck out at the pipe line. His demeanor spoke to his anger level. The phone, glued to his ear hadn't left it for 20 minutes solid. "Just a damn minute here. I'm the one hanging out there. I'm the one they interviewed about the bitch. If you think I'm taking the rap for you, you're smoking your own product. You get off your high horse and get up here so we can talk about this. I also have something for you when you get here. It'll be worth your while to get some fresh air for a change. You got 30 minutes."

"Thirty minutes. I can't get away that quick. I don't jump when you say to. I'm involved in other things. You're not the only fish in the sea, buster. Now calm down. I don't like to be threatened. And certainly not by the likes of you. I'll see what I can do to get out of here. I'll call you back. You might just have to meet me somewhere." The call was terminated and Smith jumped in his truck, started the engine and spun gravel leaving the lot.

Smith pulled out his office cell phone and called Marlene to tell her he was going into town for supplies. He left the pipe line and on Hwy 89 headed south toward Chino Valley and Prescott. He turned onto Big Chino Road headed for his trailer. The set of his jaw projected his frustration and anger. He grabbed his house keys and ran into the trailer. Inside he picked up his already packed duffle bag, his 9mm Glock, rifle, and his stash. He took a minute to survey the place to see if he had left anything important before returning to his truck and heading south again.

Once in the truck, he hit redial on his cell phone. "Don't bother coming out here, I'm on my way to see you. Meet me at Frontier Village close to the statute. And bring the money." Smith disconnected and threw the cell phone on the passenger seat.

The person he called didn't even have a chance to respond to Smith. Going to the Village was a bad idea, too open and too many people, but at that point there wasn't another option. Grabbing product and money, he was on his way to the shopping center.

By the time Smith reached the Frontier Village, dark had settled. He parked so he could see the statute and watch all directions of arrival. He kept his eyes peeled for the trademark BMW. He bent down to retrieve binoculars and the passenger window shattered. Glass shards cascaded over the passenger seat and Smith. His heart jumped into overdrive, adrenaline guiding his actions. Still bent over, he started the truck, rammed it into gear and took off down the hill behind Red Lobster.

"911. What is your emergency?"

"Hey, I'm at Frontier Village and we just heard high powered rifle shots. Then some guy took off in a truck burning rubber."

"Frontier Village? That will be Tribal Police. I'll notify them. Where are you and what is your name so I can direct police to you?"

"We were at the bank there at the ATM. I'm in my car and I'm not moving until the cops get here."

"Just stay on the line with me until the police arrive. Is anyone injured?"

"How the heck do I know. I hit the ground when I heard the rifle. I don't know where it came from or who was getting shot at."

"Can you describe the pickup?"

"White, older model, long bed, probably a Ford F150, just the driver."

"Could you tell where it was going when it left the parking lot?"

"Headed east on Hwy 69."

"Hold on." Dispatch put out a BOLO on the truck and Tribal police arrived to take a report from the civilian.

Chapter 18

Smith tore up 69, grabbing his cell phone from the passenger seat. He hit redial again and was soon connected. "You mother fucker, wrong move on your part. I was ready to turn over the product and high tail it out of here. You just burned your bridges and your dope. I need that 40 grand, but I don't need the dope." Smith was sputtering he was so mad.

"Hey, wait. I just got here and there are cops everywhere. Where are you? I'll come to you."

"You mother fucker, you tried to shoot me. I'm not meeting you anywhere."

"Hold it, Smitty, what are you talking about a shooting? I just got here. I'm leaving before the cops come over here and try to talk to me. Tell me where you are and I'll come to you on your terms."

"I'm on my way out of town. There's a rock quarry out on 169. It's down Old Cherry Road about a mile and half, turn left at the dead tree and you go about two tenths of a mile. I'm going to be sitting up there with my rifle. You bring the money and put it on that make shift shooting stand. Then you turn and walk away. Come back in two hours and your dope will be there."

"Why can't you meet me? I didn't have anything to do with this shooting. How do I know you'll give me the dope for the money?"

"You don't. I guess you're going to have to trust me, just like I trust that you weren't involved in trying to kill me."

"I'm on my way. It'll take about 30 minutes to get there. Your head is all messed up. How do I know you're not going to try to shoot me?"

"You don't." Smith disconnected. He was watching his rear view mirror for signs of the Beemer and cops. He knew the last place he wanted to speed or do a traffic violation was Prescott Valley—cops there didn't play. He turned off 169 onto Old Cherry Road and bounced down the rut filled road to the turn off for the quarry. Instead of pulling in, he parked in the arroyo and hiked up the road to the quarry. He walked around the top of the quarry to a vantage point over the entrance and waited.

His whole world was caving in on him—first Marvin dogging him about irregularities and then that damn Janelle. If she hadn't started running her mouth and threatening him, she'd still be around, but no, she wanted to play house and be his partner or she'd go to the cops. Damn, nothing was working. He had a fair sized nest egg from the dope and just one more would put him in a comfortable place to get below the border and live the rest of his life a free man.

19

JOE WAS MONITORING the scanner at the bunk house when the call went out for Tribal Police at Frontier Village. He checked the make and model of Smith's truck against dispatch's. He called Oriole and Fred to alert them to the possibility of Smith's involvement. "Look, Marlene said he left the office about five minutes after we were there. His truck is a white, Ford F150. Let's meet at the Village and see if anyone can verify it's Smith." Joe could feel a resolution coming.

"Oriole, check with dispatch on the BOLO. See if we got any bites." Fred and Oriole were lights and sirens on their way to the Village. The parking lot was already filled with emergency personnel, Tribal Police, Prescott City Police, Sheriff's Office personnel and the Village security.

They didn't learn anything new from officers at the scene except they did get a partial license plate on the BMW that left shortly after the shot was fired. They added a BOLO on what they had on the Beemer. The witness identified the license plate of the truck and it was confirmed as Smith's. Contact with dispatch provided an update on the location of the truck. Prescott Valley Police had observed it on 69 proceeding south out of Prescott Valley. All units in the area were alerted to observe and report only. A sheriff's unit on 169 reported the truck was eastbound and the Beemer was sighted not too far behind. A complete license plate was provided by the sheriff's unit and the car came back registered to Gary Patterson of Prescott.

"I told you Patterson was too slick for my liking. He's up to his neck in this. He might even have been the one to eliminate Stutz." Fred did an I told you so with his right eye brow.

"But what's his connection to Smith, drugs? It makes no sense. Why jeopardize a career for drugs?" Oriole struggled with the identification they had received.

"Well, we have Patterson at the Village and on the 169 and we have Smith at the Village and on 169. I'd say there is a direct connection of something. Remember when Patterson paled during the interview? Maybe, just maybe he really didn't know about the death of Stutz. Maybe that's why he was so surprised. But why eliminate Janelle? There must be something else we don't know, a missing piece that ties her to Smith or Patterson and they had to get rid of her. We may never have that if we can't get Patterson or Smith to pony up." Fred was talking through his thoughts on the problem they faced as they sped down the highway.

Smith had worked his way to the top of the quarry and concealed himself on a ledge so he wasn't back lit by the moon. As he waited, he plotted his next move after getting the money from Patterson. Off in the distance he heard the approach of a vehicle. He readied his rifle and scope in the shooting stand.

Patterson turned off the main road and drove slowly over the ruts to avoid damage to his prize BMW. He stopped at the turnoff, killed the engine and lights, remaining in his car for five minutes to let the noise settle in the darkness. He turned off the interior light switch so the overhead lights would not come on, and got out very quietly. Knowing Smith was already at the quarry, he moved off the road and walked toward the quarry. He circled around the parking area to a knoll where he could observe the quarry. In his left hand, he carried the money Smith had demanded, in his right he carried the rifle he had recently fired. He stopped frequently to listen and watch the area for any signs of movement, knowing that Smith was concealed somewhere nearby. He allowed his eyes to adjust to the darkness hoping to see where Smith was hiding, but all he saw was the quarry, the ridge and the mesquite bushes.

Suddenly, the night was transfixed by the sound of gunshots. Patterson flattened himself to the sandy ditch dropping the money and bringing the rifle up ready. All he could see was the quarry, no Smith, no gun, no nothing. He inched forward on his elbows imbedding gravel in his forearms. Looking over the edge of the ditch, he caught movement to the right and off about 50 yards. He could see a person in a crouched run moving to his left searching back and forth. Patterson thought it looked like Smith, but in the limited light and these conditions he wasn't positive.

Smith had watched Patterson's arrival from on top the quarry and decided to move down the back side of the hill to provide a welcome committee. He arrived in the wash about the same time he saw Patterson get out of the Beemer. Smith waited until he could see Patterson's outline against the moonlit sky and then brought his rifle up to his shoulder. Smith figured to get the money and get out before the cops arrived and if that meant leaving Patterson dead or dying, so be it. Patterson had already betrayed him and tried to take him out. Turnabout was fair play as far as Smith was concerned.

Smith took aim at where he thought Patterson might be hiding and let off one round, moved to the left and let off a round and swung to the right and let off a third round. Either he would get close enough to hit Patterson or scare him into remaining where he was hiding. Either way it got Smith closer to Patterson's car and in accurate shooting distance of Patterson. Smith moved on a belly crawl through the wash avoiding the sagebrush and cactus, maintaining quiet as much as he could. He poked his head up in time to see Patterson, 20 feet away, reach into his car. Smith crawled the last 15 feet of the wash to come up behind the BMW.

Patterson held onto his rifle and the pistol he got out of the car and dropped to the ground using the car as shelter. He listened to the darkness hoping for a sound that would alert him to Smith's whereabouts. He knew his ill placed shots had created this situation and didn't plan on repeating that mistake. He'd taken one life; he had no compunction about taking another for his survival. Playing gay to get closer to the deal coming down at the pipeline proved laborious and fatal for Marvin, but financially rewarding. Except now he had to deal with Smith.

Smith took careful aim at the shadow Patterson presented and shot for his leg. The resounding boom rang in his ears as he watched Patterson fall to the ground and scream in pain.

Patterson grabbed his rifle from the ground where it had fallen, rolled over and aimed in the direction of the shot that had entered his left calf. His shot went wild, but caused Smith to flatten behind the car. Patterson could feel the blood running down his leg into his boot. He knew he needed to get attention immediately and also knew he couldn't get out without taking care of Smith first.

Smith eased around the front of the car being careful to step quietly. He was positive he had struck Patterson, but wasn't sure of the damage. His goal was to get done fast and get the money and drugs and get out. He raised up at the driver's side front bumper to see Patterson facing away from him.

Patterson lay on his right side wrapping his belt around the bleeding wound hoping to staunch the flow. His thoughts were racing: shoot Smith, get out of here go back east, go south to Mexico. He was thinking so hard, he failed to take notice of the approach by Smith.

Smith lifted the .22 and carefully took aim at Patterson's broad back, took in a breath and squeezed the trigger. The shot entered Patterson's upper back ripping its way through the lung causing internal hemorrhaging. Smith waited a minute to see if Patterson was still a danger to him, walked up to the dying Patterson and smiled.

"You mother fucker, I told you not to ever double cross me and we'd do fine. Instead what'd you do, try to set me up for Stutz's murder." Smith grabbed Patterson's shoulder and his rifle and rolled him over on his back. "Where's the money and meth?"

"I'm dying. I can't breathe." Blood tinged with air bubbles oozed out his lips. "I didn't bring the money or meth. You killed me for nothing."

Smith opened the driver's door and searched the front seat for his booty. Finding nothing in the front, he leaned over the back seat looking for the money and drugs. "You fucker. I'd better find it or I'll make you into a pin cushion." He backed out of the car, kicked Patterson on his way to the trunk. He opened the hatch, found a blue tarp, lifted it and underneath found his treasure. He grabbed the briefcase and turned to leave.

Patterson had rolled up into a sitting position propped against the BMW. He reached into his left inside coat pocket and pulled out a snub nosed .38. He crossed his arms over his stomach, left over right to conceal the gun. "Smith, you can't just leave me here, you gotta call the police so they'll come find me."

"Now that's just what I'm going to do. Put my neck in a noose for your rotten hide." Smith said as he rounded the back end of the car and peered at Patterson.

Patterson took careful aim and shot Smith in the chest, once, twice, before Smith fell face first in the dirt. Patterson reached into his right coat pocket and pulled out his cell phone. He dialed 911.

"911 what is your emergency?"

"I've been shot. I shot him back. I'm dying. I'm out on Old Cherry Road. It was self-defense." Choking on his own blood, he tried again to talk to the operator. "I thought I knew who killed Stutz and confronted the weasel, but he out smarted me. He lured me into an ambush. Send help." Patterson laid the cell phone down with the line still open hoping emergency personnel would triangulate and get to him.

Fred and Oriole got the relay that their subjects were somewhere on Old Cherry Road. Fred called for backup and drove like a bat out of Hell to the coordinates dispatch provided from the open cell phone line. When they arrived, they cut their lights, got out, and carefully crept up on the scene.

"Police." Fred announced as he shone his flashlight on the scene. Oriole had moved off to the left and rear of the BMW and had her Glock out with her flashlight in her left hand.

"You take Smith, I got Patterson." Fred whispered as he walked up to Patterson and kicked the .38 away, then bent down and checked for a pulse.

Oriole kicked the rifle away from Smith, placed her fingers on his carotid artery and found no pulse. "Smith's dead. What's Patterson's status?"

"I got a faint pulse. Call for paramedics. I'll check him for other weapons."

"Patterson. Tell me what happened."

Patterson strained to talk as blood oozed, "Smith was going crazy, he shot me. I fired in self-defense. He was blackmailing me."

"Who killed Stutz? Come on Patterson who killed Marvin?"

"Smith. He killed Janelle and Stutz. He was running drugs through Yavapai County and Stutz found out." Patterson coughed and more blood dribbled down his chin.

"Why were you involved? What were you doing with Smith? I found the briefcase with the money. What's that all about?"

"Smith wanted the money tonight. I brought it to him. He killed me. I'm dying. I know it."

"Paramedics were called; they'll be here in a minute. Talk to me. Tell me what was going on. It'll be good to clear your soul. There's more to this than you're telling us. I know you were running drugs with Smith. I know Smith killed Janelle, but he didn't kill Stutz. You did. Didn't you?" Fred was talking fast holding his recorder close to Patterson's lips.

"How did you find out? How did you know? It was an accident. Then Smith got scared and wanted to hide the body so it wouldn't be connected to our operation. We had a good thing going." He coughed again."We were making about 50 grand a month, socking it away. Planning to move away from here as soon as I figured I had enough." Another cough and Patterson paled. "Meth came in almost every other day. We ran it out north 89 and across Jerome to Camp Verde, north to Flagstaff and points east or south to Phoenix and points east and west. We were set to make millions and Stutz found out 'cause Smith got stupid and careless. I met up with Stutz to see what he knew. He thought I was gay like he was. He figured Smith was running drugs. We had to eliminate him. Then Janelle put 2 and 2 together and Smith did her." Patterson fell over on his side and blood drained from his mouth.

Oriole had used her walkie talkie and to talk to paramedics and gave a brief summary of the situation to dispatch. Paramedics arrived in less than five minutes from the Dewey Humboldt station, but Patterson was dead by the time they pulled up.

Oriole and Fred began processing the scene for evidence. They went back to the office, wrote up their reports, called Joe and let him know the status and went home.

Over cold beer, they debriefed the two cases. "Fred, there has to be more to running drugs. Where does JD fit in? How did Smith and Patterson hook up? What did Janelle find out?" Oriole was processing information and looking at all the unanswered questions.

20

BACK AT THE RANCH, Summer had put supper on hold, and provided snacks while waiting for Oriole and Fred to make it back to the war room. Joe, Marlowe, Chalcey and Summer were ready for Fred and Oriole when they drove in the yard, knowing a case had been solved and they'd be able to take some time to relax for a few days. Salads of every kind were on the huge dining room table: Chinese cabbage, potato salad, tossed salad and fruit salad. Cold cuts were in the frig waiting with all the condiments. Beer and wine were cooling.

"Oriole, Uncle Fred. Tell us. Tell us. Come on give it to us." Chalcey was begging for all the gory details.

"Hi, honey. Nothing to tell. Case closed. You'll read about it tomorrow. Let's eat. Tell me about your day. What did you and Summer do while Marlowe was saving criminals?" Oriole wrapped her arms around her daughter and squeezed.

"Oriole, you stop talking that way to my granddaughter. My clients are not criminals. They are people who are entitled to representation and can't afford to hire Jerry Spence." Marlowe circled both her daughter and granddaughter with her arms.

Joe looked at Oriole and Chalcey as they hugged and missed the closeness of family.

Summer stood back, wiped her hands on a tea towel, and

assessed her descendants with a calculating knowledge that these women, old and young, were solid, loving, honest and wholesome.

The respect and love that permeated the house reminded Summer of early days with her mother and father and she silently said a blessing in their honor.

www.ingramcontent.com/pod-product-compliance
Lightning Source LLC
Chambersburg PA
CBHW070630130626
46555CB00006B/2509